MIRRORS

MIRRORS

Mirrors lie,
they do not show you
what is inside.

Carol M Simon

PARTRIDGE

To order additional copies of this book, contact
Toll Free 800 101 2657 (Singapore)
Toll Free 1 800 81 7340 (Malaysia)
orders.singapore@partridgepublishing.com

www.partridgepublishing.com/singapore

'Mirrors, it does not always reflect what you want to see'

I would like to thank everyone who supported me in every way possible, especially my parents, Uncle Kevin, my godparents, my nieces and nephew and best friends. Also, thank you to everyone that was involved in this process.

I write because it is a must, it is a passion. I write every day to understand how far I have come and how far could I go.

This was something that was playing in my mind for quite some time, it is something short and simple for you to enjoy.

Hopefully this is a beginning for more to come.

Prologue

I knocked at the top of the coffin as hard as I could, I was stuck alive in a coffin, and I was sweating nervously, screaming in pain and fear. What if I never made it out alive from here today? What about my baby, I will never be able to see my unborn baby. My baby would not be able to see his or her father. I never made it to even one ultrasound to find out how my baby was doing. I felt guilty and sad; I could never be a good mother figure.

I had so many unwanted thoughts in my head, which I could not allow it turn into reality. I screamed once more louder than before, I was sure this coffin was not buried six feet under this ground; he was not strong and smart enough to do it.

This was the best he could do, I smiled wickedly at that thought, and this was how he wanted to end this game between us.

I looked at the left corner, there was a small mirror. I moved my arm a little and picked it up. Using my other arm, I wiped the dry blood off my lips and dusted off the sand off my eyes. I closed my eyes shut, I wish this was all just a dream, I should not have said a word to him on the first day I met him. Like people would say curiosity killed the cat indeed. I held the mirror tight in my hands. I had a thing for mirrors, whether it was a compact one, a huge antique one, I have always adored it all. People always found it to be a strange obsession, my brother was obsessed with cars, my niece was into dolls and there was me.

I have always believed that mirrors do not always show what you want to see. My dad once told me when you are sad, look into a mirror and smile; you will no longer see that sad face of yours. It makes you believe things that you want to see. That was the sad truth about mirrors. Ever since he said those words to me, I took it as a personal way to make myself feel better whenever I knew something was wrong.

I opened my eyes and I looked into that small mirror, it was so dark in here, there was a ray of light poking through where the nails in the woods were. I could see the right side of my face. I have heard people say that love surely hurts but I did not expect it to bring that much of damages. There is always a difference between expecting for it and preparing for it.

I would not have known that it was a way for me to find my dream man. That was one element that kept him and me together for all these months. My thoughts were all about him, how he is as a person. He was creative in his own way, but I guess I met him at the wrong time and it led to this. He could take the thoughts in your head and put it into paintings. I adored how he got lost in his work; he would sit in a corner and draw for hours, with his tongue sticking out slightly without him realizing it. He could stand in one place for hours admiring someone else's work. I would end up smiling at that sight; I knew he was not mine to keep.

His passion was brighter than fire that I have seen burning. I never realized that his hatred towards me was brighter than his passion.

Whenever I looked into the mirror, I would find him standing behind of me. He would give unexpected hugs from the back, while I got ready for my next show. Those little moments made me believe that we were meant for each other. As a child, I have always fantasied about having a husband like him, handsome, successful and loved by many. It was too good to be true when he walked into my life, I should have expected the worst.

I think most of the women around me were jealous of how he treated me, he made me like a queen, not a prince but a queen with his royal treatments, and he was the perfect gentleman. I have always joked around saying that I never deserved it, but he would always remind me by saying "You are a princess to me…" That statement made me feel special. Not everything special last forever unfortunately. I thought to myself, maybe this was all a cruel joke on me.

You must be wondering, who is this artist that I am describing about, who was I to him and to the world?

Let me bring you into the past, and I will tell you how I ended up here in the future, in a coffin.

I closed my eyes tight. Reliving all those sweet memories that slowly turned bitter.

TO BEGIN WITH

"AVIS! AVIS!" I heard my name being called out at the end of the corridor and I walked towards it, leaning against these rough walls killed my back. I nodded at the nurse at the counter and she stared at me with an unhappy face. Of course, I guess her husband must have visited me at the club before. I shrugged as I looked at her, "your grandmother is in room 79" and just like that she walked away from me.

I had to find that room by myself. I turned and walked a little further down the corridor and my grandmother walked out from that room. She smiled, she was the one person that loved me and accepted me for who I was in life. It was not something that she could talk to the other old folks about while sipping on a cup of tea, but hey at least I was still surviving and on my own. That was surely something she could be proud of.

She sat down quietly on the chair outside, the place was surrounded by plants and colorful flowers and it seemed very homely, something that I never had and never would. I smiled at her waiting for her to say something.

"That college that you were speaking of...."

I took a deep breath in and let it out, I shook my head, and it was a sign that I have not enrolled myself in that college or any other colleges. My grandmother sighed at that, I knew she was somehow disappointed in my choice but she never really said anything to it.

She raised me up after my mother left me when I was about five years old, my dad was in prison for some reason and apparently I have a brother, which I had never heard about. I wanted her to be proud of me, I want her to look at me as a successful person, watch me get married and have kids for her to play with. I wanted her to see that I could have a family of my own. At this point, I could only get rid of these dreams, I was a dancer at a famous club in the city, I had no plans to go to college just yet and my grandmother was stuck in an old folk's home, which surprisingly she was happy about.

Some fairytale I was living in. I rolled my eyes at that thought.

"I am not going to be here forever, and I hope you know that." And with those last words, she got up from her seat and walked away quietly. Seemed like everyone has a habit of walking away from me.

I got up from my seat as well, prepared to walk back to the club which was not far away from this place. I kept my hands warm inside my pockets. I lowered my head as I walked out from the home. Her words haunted my thoughts as I was walking. It was scary to know that one day the person that I loved the most, would be gone. She always asked to be criminated, because she was afraid to be buried, she had the thought what if she wakes up and finds herself in a coffin. I smiled lightly, that thought of hers always made me laugh when I was younger, but as she grew older and I did too, those thoughts were not something to laugh about anymore together.

I wanted to fix my life, I was turning twenty-four soon, and I joined the club as an exotic dancer when I was seventeen. I remembered begging Antony; he was the owner of the club. I was under-aged and I wanted to join his line of exotic dancers. I did not want to do anything out of my will, I only wanted to dance and when Antony took me in, he made sure taking care of me was top on his priority list. I was lucky, after this job, I had money to rent an apartment for myself; I had money to buy food and clothes, something which my parents had never provided me with. It is a tough life which I am only trying to survive in.

I walked into the club and Antony greeted me, he was holding an envelope and handed it over to me. I tore it open and took out the papers, it was another set of contract, I looked up at him and he was already staring at me.

"It is for you to renew the contract, with a raise" I was not a person who spoke that much, I raised up my left eyebrow and I knew he understood what I meant.

"Many of the customers have requested for you lately, you deserve a raise" He smirked.

"I will hand it in later..." He knew I would extend my stay here. What will I do other than this job, like the Joker once said 'if you are that good at something, do not do it for free'

I pushed the pink curtains aside; it gave me goose bumps, I hated bright colors. I wore black 90% of the time. I sat in my chair, threw the papers on my dressing table and covered my face. I took a deep breath in and let it out. I needed a cigarette; I needed some space from everyone.

I uncovered my face, letting my eyes to get used to the lights again. I saw the application letters it arrived as well, different colleges with the same course offered. I was interested in journalism. It was something I want to take on since I was younger, pretending the wooden spoon was a microphone to interview people from the neighborhood. I smiled at those memories, but the smile was quick to disappear when I caught a glimpse of the contract to stay at this club. I could never make good choices.

"Let life do its thing" I turned around it was Sharon; she is one of the dancers around here. "Worrying will never help you to make better decisions" I nodded to what she had to say "It would only make things blurry" and she took a seat next to me.

"I never made the right choice in life" I whispered only for the both of us to hear. I did not want her to feel sorry for me; I needed her to help me somehow to make a good choice for once.

"If you do not take the risk, trust me you will never find out what the outcome may be" She always had the right words to tell someone. Maybe it was because she was a mother to three kids; this was her job in order to feed her kids. I nodded at her

"Thank you Sharon" I knew what to do for now, I grabbed a pen from the table and opened the envelope; I took out the contract and flipped the pages slowly looking through it, a few words capturing my eyes here and there. I set the papers down and signed it.

I got up from my seat, prepared to hand in the letters to Antony but my phone rang interrupting my thoughts.

"Hello is this Avis Torres?" a voice spoke as I answered the call, "Yes, this is her" it sounded like an elderly woman "Your grandmother has been admitted into the intensive care unit" but I just met her earlier, how did this happen so quickly "She has been complaining about chest aches and now it has gotten worse…. Hello? Hello, Miss Avis?" No words left my mouth. I ended the call and walked out of the dressing room.

"Antony, here are the papers." I gave him the papers, and he smiled happily, he will be able to see me in this club for more years to come. I grabbed Sharon's handbag "Where do you think you are going woman?"

"For a drink, come on!" she shook her head as she walked out and we waved at Antony. He could never handle us both together.

We walked out, greeting everyone with a smile, we walked in silence until a little child ran up to us, "you are very beautiful" he turned towards Sharon "and so are you" and he ran off to his mother in a blink of an eye. I shook my head and giggled, that compliment was very genuine. Something that cannot be found in this world nowadays.

We walked towards the café and pushed the doors open, we sat by the windows looking through the windows, I could see my reflection; I pushed my bangs aside and tighten up the ribbon on my head. I sat back and waited for the waiter to get our orders.

I knew I had to think about my grandmother, which will require more money for her treatments, and her medications. I felt guilty knowing I ended the call with the nurse. I did not mean to do so, I panicked.

"I asked for more sugar! Is that so hard to understand?" I heard a deep, rough voice shouting at the barista, bringing me out of my thoughts. I could not see the person properly, but his voice was surely something to remember. After all it is just sugar, be more polite, I thought to myself.

"Well would you look at that, rich man making a scene" Sharon sighed as she rested her head against the window. I turned towards the scene again, he grabbed the packet of sugar and walked out, and he was wearing a blue long sleeved shirt, sleeves rolled up with fitted black jeans. He looked quite good from what I could see. I shook my head "Quick get me some coffee" I pointed at the counter "we need to get back before the clients arrive" Sharon smiled at me as she got up from her seat.

I turned to look out of the window again, there was that guy again. I could only see his back; he crossed the busy streets and disappeared. Sharon brought us coffee and we were ready to leave the café. The entire time, I could feel my phone vibrating in my pocket. I was in no mood to talk to anyone right now.

I am always known as the person with a few words. I never really had friends while growing up; I was not forced to be in any situations where I should be talking to people. I chose not to. I liked my space. I grabbed my cup and we walked out slowly enjoying the breeze. It was getting colder as the sun was ready to set in.

I looked at up from the ground, and all I could see was happy couples, they were holding hands, kissing each other, talking about their future I suppose.

"Good luck you love birds!" I shouted from across the street. Sharon was laughing hysterically

"You have finally lost it" She looked at me and shook her head.

I took a sip of my coffee, and we continued our journey back to the club. The Exotic Life club was our home, we found our family in there, and we found money and happiness as well. I rather be here than anywhere else. I smiled as we reached the club, I threw the cup in the bin and Sharon did the same.

"Right on time, we have a long night ahead" Antony was walking around, he gave us a slight smile, I had to prepare myself for tonight. I pushed the curtains aside; the room was crowded with all the performers.

"Look who is here, the one who will never-" I had no time to listen to what my haters had to say to me and more importantly about me. "Save it Mel, not today" I walked over to my seat and took out my make-up sets. I applied the foundation and continued with it, as I looked into the mirror, I took a deep breath in and let it out slowly. I applied some purple lipstick, and I got up from my seat.

I pushed the curtains and Low Life by The Weeknd was blaring through the speakers. It was just too loud, it made us hyper. I went to the bar side prepared to serve the customers with their orders. A young looking guy knocked over a few of the glasses. He was intoxicated. I could sigh because someone had to clean up that mess and that was not going to be me. I made him sit down on the stool properly and he tried to plant one on my lips, I backed off a little.

"You look really beautiful…" He slurred

"and you are really done, thank you" I smiled and he held my hand and asked for another drink even leaving the bartender to shake his head at this sight.

"Are you seeing anyone?" He asked me while I wiped the counter. I pulled the cup away from him and kept it aside.

"What seems to be the real problem here?" I knew something was going on with this boy and he sighed

"She was talking about weddings, she asked me when were we going to settle down, I got really nervous and she got so I left" I was trying to catch on to every word he was saying to me with all the loud song playing in the background made me think sometimes I have a hearing problem.

"Ah boys and marriages" I smirked and took a napkin to wipe his face. He was a good looking guy, he had nothing to worry about, if only he had a good heart to match his looks.

"Look, if it was meant to be, it will be" I took the stool nearby and pushed it near me to sit down next to him. "if she was made for you, no matter where you are or how many years go by she will come back to you, she will be there for you" I kept my hand on his left shoulder and rubbed it a little hoping he would feel better.

"Listen, I am not going to tell you that there are many fishes in the sea for you to choose from" He looked up at me with his teary eyes "because she just might be the sea for you"

"enough to drown me Miss…" he rubbed his face probably hoping this would just end.

"or enough to swim" I smiled hoping he would catch on.

"You know she is right" The bartender spoke from behind the counter, nodding and cleaning up the glasses.

I giggled "So get off this chair, go with the flow and just do not rush, things will fall into place for you"

He smiled "Thank you Miss" he gave me a tight hug and "You!" he said that while pointing at the bartender and he returned a wink as a you are welcome sign.

Goodness me! I felt like I was someone's therapist. Look at me giving relationships advice while I struggled with my own. I chuckled and continued to clean up the mess on the counter. I high fived the bartender.

I walked around the club and I saw the back of guy facing the counter, he was ordering a couple of drinks.

I have heard that rough voice somewhere. It was that guy who demanded sugar from that café earlier today. Boy oh boy, I thought to myself, the bartender better be on his best behavior with this man. He wore that same fitted jeans and I smiled. He turned around and my breath was taken away. That sounded cliché, but he looked like a Hollywood movie star. He had tattoos covering up his arm where his rolled up shirt left off. He had slicked back hair and a well grown beard more like a scruff. He looked much older than I expected. I found myself staring at him for quite some time. I smiled to myself; he had bright green eyes from I what could gather.

"Avis, sweetheart!" Sharon's voice brought me back from my thoughts and I looked at her "There will be someone arriving, could you welcome him?" I nodded and lowered my head as I pushed through the crowd. I felt his green eyes were on me.

I stepped out, waited patiently for whoever I was supposed to. I am lucky to be a part of this club, they have many beautiful girls, dancing, entertaining and then there is me. I am more towards a couch potato. I looked around, looked at my watch, and few of the customers inside were outside now as well, smoking their cigarettes. I licked my lips and I felt someone grab my wrist.

"How about you follow me?" A strange looking guy was smiling at me, "How about you let go of me?" I caught a glimpse of those green eyes again behind this stranger. Whoever this was, he held my wrist tighter. I grabbed his arm and twisted it. He struggled a little before he got out of it. I grabbed him by the head and threw him over my shoulder unto the hard ground.

I was panting heavily "I suggest you get home" he wiggled on the ground whining in pain.

"Not again Avis!" Antony came out with a few others "No No No!" I giggled at his reaction; this was not my first time throwing men over my shoulders, besides they deserved it if they misbehaved. "You should have been the bouncer here" Antony told me as he passed through, one of the bouncers gave me a high five. I dusted the dirt of my blouse.

"Pretty impressive I must say" those were last words I heard, before I ended my night.

I hugged my pillow as I opened my eyes; the sun was shining right on my face. I sighed as I grabbed my phone; it had a miss call from the old folk's home. I dialed the number again and waited for someone to answer it "Yes Miss Avis" it was that nurse that hated me for no apparent reason. "The home called me several times and I am-"

Before I could finish my sentence, she mentioned something that would forever haunt me "Your grandmother passed away yesterday night"

My brain could not process this, how could something like this happen, I saw her yesterday, she was perfectly alright "She had a heart attack" She needs to be here, she needed to see her great grandchildren, she was my only support system. What was I to do without her? I ended the call. I grabbed a pillow and covered my face as I cried into it. I had no one to call as my family, I was all alone now. I screamed as loud as I could, my phone vibrated. I threw the pillow across my room and picked it up. I had a new friend request. I clicked on the profile as I wiped away my tears, his name is Alexander Jayden.

Those bright green eyes belonged to this man. I clicked on a picture; this man was thoroughly a gift from God. I could not see any flaws; he was perfect as I continued to browse through. The way he dressed was neat and he had a lot of followers. I accepted his request; I was also prepared to get to the club. I guess I needed to make some extra cash tonight; I needed to handle my grandmother's funeral.

I wonder where my mother was, the last time I heard from a friend, she was doing alright. I guess she married some rich man and settled down with a new family. She could not take care of me, but she was prepared to take care of a newborn. I just wished she would not destroy the baby's life. Somehow that baby had the same blood as me; I was so willing to look after.

I wanted to cry for a few hours straight, just thinking about my life was enough to cause tsunami.

I changed my clothes and washed my face. I grabbed my bag and locked the doors. "Good morning Avisa" Mr. Francis wished me as I walked down the stairs

"It is Avis!" I smiled as I passed by.

The sun was shining brighter than before, I looked at my watch, it was already in the afternoon, no wonder I was hungry. I walked towards the club, and it was closed. I tried pushing the doors, it was locked. Antony must be running late. I shrugged, I looked over at the corner, there was man lying down. I sat down carefully beside him; I did not want to wake him up. I took out my earphones and plugged them in. I played a couple of songs as I looked at the people that passed by me.

Some looked happy to where they were heading, some looked depressed. I hugged my knees; a woman was shouting at her child, a man kissed his wife's baby bump, a woman crying walking far away from her boyfriend I suppose.

"Everyone is busy creating a life of their own" I jumped slightly hearing that voice. The man next to me woke up, I nodded as I continued looking at the people around me "Maybe someday it will be better, it might not be today"

I sighed "But some day right?" I turned to him as I talked to him and he smiled. "I am no beggar; my son kicked me out of his home a few days ago"

I was surprised to hear those words but seems like this man was not. "I expected this to happen, but I was not prepared for it" There was a difference between expecting and preparing. He had tears forming in his eyes. "I know there will be something good out of this" how could he be so positive at such moment, "Hopefully it will be for you too" He grabbed his brown sack and got up. I could not see his face properly as the sun shinned, he gave me one more smile as he walked away from me.

I heard keys rattling and it was Antony opening up the club. How fast can a moment pass by, leaving us speechless to embrace it. I sighed as I got up as well.

I went into the club, prepared to perform as early as I could, there were already customers throwing money at me; I picked it all up, note by note and kept it in my pockets. I took turns with the other dancers, I cleared my pockets as another danced on the stage, I checked my phone for any new messages and turns out I did receive one from Alexander, I opened it and it read

I can see you

I looked around and I could not find him, a hand grabbed my shoulders and I jumped a little, "It's just me" I raised my left eyebrow "and I could have hit you" I crossed my arms

"One dance for me" He pulled me out from the backstage area, he sat down in an empty chair, and he licked his lips as he waited for another song to be played. He watched me carefully, I felt nervous, Ride by Ciara blared through the speakers, my heartbeat increased as I could feel the beat of the song. I embraced the song as I danced for him. No I do not plan to strip, He brought me closer to where he was, "I am sorry for your loss" I knew what he meant, but how did he know? I stared at him blankly for a few seconds and I am sure he felt confused by just looking at my expression. I sighed; well rich people had their ways of finding out information, why would I bother asking something when I probably knew the answer to it.

I continued dancing, and he reached into his pockets, he took a large amount of money out from his wallet. He kept it in my pocket. "Use it for the funeral" He got up and gave me a slight kiss on my cheek.

"I can't just take our money" I held the money tighter in my hands "Not like this" I shook my head; this would be enough to settle the funeral, and those lists of medication bills.

"You do need it, if you need more" I could not let him finish; he cannot just give cash to some stranger, that was just ridiculous. "Keep the money, and how would you like to put this behind you"

He was already trying to find a way to make me feel better, after everything that has happened for the past few days, which I assumed he would have found out as well. I smiled at that thought. I should be finding ways to keep myself happy.

"My friend is having a mini get together" and I knew he was prepared to roll his eyes. I giggled slightly and he pushed a stray of my light brown hair behind my left ear.

"I am too old for those kinds of things" I was afraid to ask how old he was. Deep down, I kept saying to myself that age is just a number. I was hoping he would say yes and just follow me to this mini party; I see it as an opportunity to find out who this man really was.

He got up and nodded at me, we were going after all, "Wait here while I grab my bag" I ran backstage pass those curtains, and pushed my lipstick, purse and anything important I could find on the table, into my handbag. I dashed right back out before anyone could ask me any questions, I grabbed his hand and we both pushed through the crowd and got out.

He walked me towards his car, it looked beautiful, and like any gentleman would do he opened the door for me and I got in. We drove off to my friend's place, with the windows rolled down, singing off key to some country songs playing on the radio, we even stopped to get food. I felt like I was creating memories as a teenager, something that I have never done.

"Avisa Avisa beautiful Avisa" Anna shouted as she greeted us at the front door.

"You are just the same as that old man living in my block" I sighed as I pushed her aside and went in, the crowd was pretty wild, with red cups in their hand, yes we knew what was in it. I was starting to think that I was kind of old for this thing.

"Thought you said this was a get together" his voice brought me back to where we were, "what were you expecting Alex?" I looked around scanning through the teenagers dancing around; more like on each other if that was possible "People sipping on a cup of coffee talking about life?" I shook my head and chuckled "surely you won't be able to find that here"

It was his turn to smirk, I rose up my hand to touch his scruff, I wanted to feel how that was against the palm of my hand, and I got dragged away by Anna and a couple of other girls.

"Tell me who is that good looking man that you have brought over" I do not even know how to answer those girls.

"Alexander, that's his name" I kept my eyes on the ground as the girls were talking about him, Anna looked at me, she had that curious but confused look on her face. "Why?" I mouthed that word to her. She came closer to me, "He does not look like someone that you would date"

I turned around and I saw Alex, he was trying to keep a conversation with someone who was clearly drunk. He seemed quite out of place here. I tilted my head slightly, he was not the number one in my list to date kind of guys, but that list could change.

"He is not, he is just someone I am getting to know" Anna sighed "That is all" I reassured her, I think I was trying to convince myself more than her.

I grabbed a cup and walked over to him "Want some?" That sounded cheesy but it was the drink that I was talking about. He shook his head and kept his eyes on me while I took a sip.

"How about you answer some questions that I have?" I was trying to make it sound like a question; I wanted his permission before I could ask anything.

"Sure, go ahead" I took a deep breath in and let it out, well this was the opportunity that I was finding for, why was I nervous, maybe I did not expect him to say yes that fast.

"How old are you really?" I looked at him

"I am 41 years old, I am about to turn 42 soon" That was unexpected; he seemed younger than he had mentioned. I guess he was like wine; you get better as you grow older.

"How or why did you find me?" I took another sip from my cup.

"My colleague brought me to that club a few weeks ago, and I saw you" I smiled widely at him "You were breath taking on that stage, you stood out from all the other girls there"

My eyebrows were pushed together in confusion "How so?"

"You do not do things that you are not comfortable with, I found that out through Antony, he could not stop talking about you" I nodded as a sign for him to go on "I found you and I got your number, here we are" He took the cup out of my hands and kept it aside.

I threw my right arm around his shoulder, he let out a manly laugh at my action, "Get up, let's go to the park"

He seemed taken back with the idea, he looked at the watch, I took a peak at it, it was almost past midnight. He got up, I smiled following him and off we were to the park.

I laid down on the grass, looking up at the stars, it was cold I could feel the cold breeze against my skin giving me goose bumps, he laid next to me. "I have never done this, it is nice"

I smirked but something interesting caught my eye, it was shining under the lights of the stars. I tore eyes away from that sight and looked back up at the stars hoping to push that thought away.

"Wouldn't you like to know about me?" I smiled and he nodded in excitement. "Well, I have a little bit of India and Puerto Rico in me."

He tilted his head towards the right in wonder and amazement. "No way that is even possible…"

"My dad has half of it and my mum has the other half, and they combined it, there is me" I smiled because deep down that was about it which I knew about my parents.

"No wonder you look exotic" I laughed at his statement. "I mean it! Not only an exotic dancer but exotic looks too" He smirked at me "an exotic body as the bonus" It was his turn to laugh as I hit his shoulder slightly.

"What about you?" I asked him

"That is for you to find out…"

I shook my head listening to his answer.

"It is peaceful here" I hummed at what he said and I heard him laugh a little which caused me to do the same. Surely by now I think the universe would know I do not do anything related to romance, I would be the last person someone would ask for a relationship advice. We both lay enjoying the cold wind and the quietness was comforting. Things were already starting to change up these past few days. I felt his hands on mine, I turned my head to look at him, his eyes sparkled as he inched closer, he gently gave a kiss on my cheek, and a peck on my lips. He was even shyer than I thought; he kissed me, his lips lingering on mine longer.

"I would like to thank everyone who is present here today" I wiped away my tears, as I looked at the coffin being lowered down into the ground. I dropped a rose before they could start lowering the soil.

I remembered about every small thing that she has done for me, like ironing my clothes, cook for me when I was younger and work two to three jobs a week to keep a roof on our heads. The one particular memory that I have cherished was when in elementary school, the teacher was mean to me in the classroom.

I remembered crying and running into her arms after school. I was complaining so much and would not let her feed me because I was throwing a tantrum like any kid would at that stage. Grandma as I would call her, got dressed and brought me along to have a small talk with that teacher. She told the teacher to be a little nicer to me, because I was a sweet angel in her eyes.

She was an entire family that I have never had.

I walked away slowly, sobbing; I could not control my tears. I wanted to sit in a place where I could cry for hours, cry my heart out and not worry about it later on. I took out my phone from the pocket, I texted Alex wondering if he would want to go out.

I walked a little further, found this cute restaurant, I pushed the doors open and I took a seat waiting for someone to take my order, I pulled out my phone, still no replies from him, I sighed. I heard the chair in front of me being dragged, I looked up and it was Evan.

Evan and I went out a couple years back, I would not say we dated, it was a horrible thing we had going on. I met him through a friend, we hit off straight away, he was a sweet talker, brought me gifts unexpectedly and more. Then, he was a little physically abusive, I ran away from him one day that was the last I have heard from him.

"You look more beautiful than the last time" he gave me one of his famous smiles. I smiled back "Thank you"

I had a confused look on my face which I assumed he could understand "I just wanted to say Hi, no worries"

I could understand where he was coming from, I did not want to chase him away that easily for no apparent reasons, and the waiter took our orders and brought us our food. We ended up talking for a few hours, just catching up on each other lives since we left. He seemed like he was doing pretty well from what I could hear, he bought a new house and a car. All he needed was a family, just like me.

I took a glimpse at my phone, there was a text from him, and I opened it.

I am stuck at work; I will see you at the club later at night.

I smiled, even with a text he could put a smile on my face, I paid for the both of us and Evan walked with me to the club, the thing about this small town is that everything is just close by, all you have to do is walk around and you will find everything you need.

Evan wanted to stay back and watch a couple of dances. I giggled asking him to enjoy the show. Certainly I do not miss us being together, I have moved on but I like the person that he has become today. It is a good change.

I changed into a leather skirt and a matching top; I walked back out pushing those ugly pink curtains aside and was greeted with a kiss on my cheek

"Sharon mentioned that you were here" I kissed his cheek as well, I wanted to introduce him to Evan, and I grabbed his wrist and brought Alex to where Evan was.

"This is Evan, he is a good friend of mine" They both shook hands and Evan begun asking questions if I was dating this man or had anything go on between us, I still found it hard to answer this kinds of questions. I was not even sure what we had going on between us.

I left both of them to have a manly conversation I supposed, I headed to the bars, and got some drinks, tonight I was going to serve drinks. I liked how Antony always allows us to change it up in here. I found this as another way to meet new people. The community always assumes people working in a bar are bad influence. They are too quick to judge way before they know what the truth is.

I felt the night passing by quite fast. All of a sudden I heard glasses being shattered on the floor, tables hitting the ground and girls screaming. I turned around by the crowd was blocking my view, I tried to push through the crowd but it seemed like no one was willing to move. Whatever it was, they had their eyes fixated on it.

"They are having a fight, I saw that guy that you were with" Sharon shouted trying to beat the loud blaring music. My eye balls were about to pop out from what I heard and the bouncer pushed through the crowd while I held his hand.

Evan and Alexander were rolling on the floor, the bouncers tore them apart, kept one aside far from the other, Antony was mumbling in fear and I was still shock.

I ran over towards Alex "Tell me, what happened?" I looked at his face and checked if he was injured badly

"He started it Avis; he had so much to say"

"He is lying!" Evan shouted from the other side. I do not care who started it, I did not want to hear anything out of it, and most importantly I did not want any of them injured. Look at the mess they have made, I walked over to Antony turned him around to face me

"Get him checked out" As I looked at Evan "And send him out after that, I will take Alex to my place"

Antony just nodded, he seemed to be in a shocked state, I am surprised that he is, things like this happen around here most of the time. Each time receiving the same reaction from the boss. I shook my head and asked Alex to follow me back. He wanted to drive us back but I insisted on walking, my place was near.

We reached in silence something I was expecting, I unlocked the door, he was still a little quiet

"I am sorry but he still started it" he whispered for the both of us to hear. I nodded as I took out the first aid kit from the top of the cabinets. I cleaned up his wounds, pieces of glasses here and there. I cleaned up the mess and threw it all. I went into my bedroom and laid down; Alex walked in after a couple of minutes and rested next to me.

"Thank you" I could feel his breath on my neck. He left butterfly kisses on my hand and neck. He turned me around to face him, I saw a smile after a long night we had, and he inched closer and closed the gap with a kiss.

I knew how that night ended; I will leave it at that.

I woke up hearing sounds from the kitchen, I went into the bathroom to freshen myself up. I could smell good home cooked food as I walked out, I could see Alex preparing breakfast, nothing too fancy but simple.

It was something special; no one has done that for me.

"How was the burial yesterday?" He had his back towards me.

"It went on smoothly, I miss her already" It still feels like it had happened too fast, but I am sure she is happier in a better place, which is just not here. I just had to accept that.

"You have a new person as your support system" He pushed slightly the plate over to me. I took a bite of the sausage and boy was it good. I hummed a little in appreciation. He chuckled

"Is the person standing in front of me?" I asked him hoping for him to say a yes but all I received was a shrug as an answer.

I was eating but my eyes were on him, he took a walk towards the collection of my mirrors. I could sense there were questions and curiosity coming.

"You are obsessed with yourself?" He asked me with his eye brow raised high and I ended up laughing really hard to that question.

"My dad always told me that mirrors lie" I took a bite of the toasted bread and continued "Mirrors never really show what is inside of a person"

"Go on I am listening..." he touched one of my antique mirrors.

"Look into one of it, tell me how you feel" I turned around watching him and his expressions.

"I feel sad right now" He turned around to face me, and I pointed my finger back to the mirror, a sign for him to turn around again.

"Smile now and look at yourself, you look happy and that sadness of yours is hidden"

Alex seemed taken back with my sentence. I am sure he knew what I meant; now he would understand my obsession with mirrors.

I was not good at hiding my feelings or just about anything, mirrors helped me practice on how to mask all of those, how to understand that everyone has their own secret agendas.

He walked towards me and gave me a hug. He kept talking about a color run marathon for the past few days now, I am sure he was really excited to attend it and he wanted me to go with him. I was more than happy to follow him; we both got changed for the event and left for it. We had to get his car from where he parked at last night.

There were many people at the marathon starting line, most of them seemed like they were in their thirties and forties. I smiled as I pushed through while holding Alex's hand, we both kept our sunglasses on.

"I am going to walk throughout this marathon" Alex said as he looked around causing me to giggle.

"Alright old man if you say so…"

"Avis I might end up being very tired"

With that the flags were waved and the sound of the bullhorn caused me to jump a little. To summarize the entire experience at the marathon, people sprinkled different colors in powder form on us. We were covered in different colors, and people shooting at us with water guns. I have never felt so happy and energetic in my entire life; I smiled genuinely throughout the entire event, I was creating wonderful new memories, and it was with this man. Actually it was because of him, he opened a new door for me, I could not be more thankful than I already was. I felt myself falling even more for him but it seemed like it was a wrong thing to do.

Why did it feel wrong? I knew I was falling in love with him; it was something I should ask myself, not now that is. Right now, this moment was perfect. The world did not matter when I was with him.

The cameraman at the end of the line took a picture of us, Alex asked for it and he gave it to me.

"I would frame this up" I said as I looked at the picture.

As the event came to an end, we ate with some of the other runners, talked with the organizers and decided at the end to head over to Alex's new apartment in town. Which was surprising because he never mentioned anything about getting a new place, not a single word, it might have slipped off his mind? I was trying to be really positive.

You know what they say; a woman in love would do anything to get it right with her man. I was on dead right on that track.

We said our goodbyes to everyone and drove off; his car was always comfortable to travel in. It was a supercool family car, with class and style. The glasses were all tinted and it was black in color. Class at its finest over here.

We were greeted by the guards as they checked for Alex's id before they allowed the car to pass through. This is must be a luxurious place. He got down and opened the door for me, that act of his never gets old. He pulled out his keys in the elevator and we got down on the eleventh floor, he was grinning like a little child, he must have been really excited when he got this new place. I shook my head as he unlocked the door; it was a beautiful apartment space with a killer view of the town.

I walked towards to wall where a few paintings caught my eyes.

"You bought all of these?" I looked at each of the paintings "It must have cost a fortune"

"Those were all painted by me" He spoke out as he poured out wine into two glasses. My jaw dropped at the sight of the paintings. There were many hung on the walls around this place.

"I am an artist I would say" He chuckled as he passed me a glass of wine, I needed it. "I paint images for a living"

"So you could take the thoughts out of my head and put it into paintings?" I titled my head a little

"That is one way to put it, I have been doing it since I was little, as I grew older, people were buying it for millions, and I made a name for myself"

I never knew this about him until now; I would have thought that he was some kind of a businessman, but an artist, that was totally unexpected

"But unique" I said that last part out loud and he gave me a slight smile

"Just like you" He walked towards a room and I followed closely behind him, there were paint brushes everywhere, papers scattered around the room, it was in a mess, a creative mess.

"This is where I usually paint; I spend most of my nights in here" He picked up a brush "Maybe one day I could paint a portrait of you"

"I would love that" I left a kiss on his cheeks.

It was a new side of him, I was starting to get to know him even better now, I appreciated that he was opening up to me. I walked around the apartment a little more before he had to drop me off at the club again, I had a long night ahead of me, this day has been amazing so far, and it could not get any better than this.

"What other kinds of paintings that you do?"

"Nude paintings" His answer was short and simple, which had me wondering about it. He seemed to catch on it. "As in there is a nude model in front of me, striking a good pose and I will paint a portrait according to it"

"Something like what Jack did in Titanic, didn't he?" I asked curiously and he nodded amused with my statement.

"Yes just like what Jack did" He ran his hand through my hair saying "Smart girl, who would have knew…"

I hit his arm and asked "Don't you feel anything if you actually did something like that?" He had his eye brow raised in wonder, and I was trying to sound as polite as possible "as in women being in the nude right near you for hours maybe…"

"My work and passion is always kept on a professional side, I will never act on it because I know that would be wrong."

He seemed firm and strict with his work ethics. But by this I also knew he had self-control. He is able to put a fine line between his work life and his needs. Not many could do that, I admired him for that. Then again, it might because of his age; he was way more matured that I could be.

"Where have you been girl?" Sharon gave me a tight hug as I laughed, Antony walked over nodding to that question.

"Well remember the guy that got into a fight?" I asked the both of them and both of them answered two different answers at the same time.

"Evan!" "Alexander!"

I face palmed myself, "I am talking about Alexander" I shook my head at the both of them and they eyes sparkled with curiosity, they wanted to know more for sure, the club needed new gossips. "We have been spending some time together, I feel like I met him for a reason"

I gracefully skipped around in the club giving out high fives; I have not seen a few of the people here in days. I had Sharon and Antony following me asking a millions of questions. "I think I might be in love with him" they both gasped and looked at each other.

"Is he treating you right?!"

"Is he ok with you working at this club?!"

"Do you know what he does for a living?!"

"How old is he?"

"Is he interested in men?" Antony's last question threw us off guard, Sharon and I looked at him, that question made us roll our eyes. I shrugged Antony off.

I understood where they were coming from, they wanted to protect me and who could blame them, they were the only people left whom I could call them as my family. I knew Alex only for a couple of weeks, and now I am really starting to get to know him for the past few days and that was about it. But wasn't that why relationships were for? Where you could build the trust and share past memories and build new ones to cherish forever. I never dated or went out with other men since I left Evan. Was I prepared mentally for another, but what if Alex thinks differently from me? What if he thinks I was just a kid playing around?

I thought back a little on what happened yesterday which was starting to spark some questions in me.

As the lights came back on, I strike a pose, I looked good doing so with my all back outfit and stunning make-up. The music stopped as well. I smiled at Alex, he was sitting down with a guy who seemed to be a talent manager.

"That's a very talented dancer, you've brought in there Alex" He spoke while fixing his reading glasses. Alex decided to speak to this person in hope he would find me a job in any of the famous dance studios that were available.

I wiped my face with a towel that I brought along. I looked at both of them talking. They were in deep thoughts and so was I. I kept the towel in my bag. I was hoping he would not change who I was. I mean I wanted to be the best version of myself for this man.

I wanted to show how proud I was to have a talented man like him. I sighed, I wanted to be myself doing so, something that he would not get.

I had so many thoughts in my mind right now with no answers, I zoned out for a few seconds, was I falling in love too fast? I thought love had no timing slapped unto it. I think I might be in love with how he treats me, yeah maybe that was it, I was in love with the feeling. No guy treated me in that way, and here comes Mister Handsome with his act of opening doors for me, buying me lunch and being protective over me.

He somewhat had every qualities a girl would die for in a man. He took matters in his hands and found new ways to make me happy; hopefully I have done the same for him.

My phone vibrated in my bag, I opened it and dug through it for my phone, I needed to clear up my handbag, and it was filled with papers and unnecessary things.

I am taking you out for a vacation.

A vacation? I thought to myself, I replied with another message *But where? For how many days?*

He replied in a few seconds. *It is a secret, you do not have to pack up for this trip!*

Well then, seems like he has this handled, I trusted him and I am sure he would not take no for an answer. I smiled and informed Antony and the others before I was about to leave.

They were reluctant to let me go, everyone had their doubts. Even I did at this point. Maybe I needed this getaway; I was complaining after all that I needed some space from everyone.

Then came in the perfect chance to take a break from dealing with what everyone had to say. I received an offer to be in a music video. I felt blessed in a way because whatever I seemed to be doing was not that bad after all, not everyone looks down on a dancer, especially one from an exotic club.

However I informed the director on an earlier note saying that I was not going to do something that I was not comfortable with in front of the cameras, which he understood and agreed to but was not happy to hear about it.

The very next day, I walked into the studio and was greeted by the director. There were people working on my make-up, there were people putting on jewelries on me even someone feeding me so I would not faint. I felt like Keri Hilson at a backstage concert. I was brought to the set, I gave my phone to one of the make-up artist asking the person to record my performance.

As the cameras rolled, I began to dance accordingly to the music that was being played. I embraced the character that I was meant to be playing in the video. After a few hours of shooting, I felt exhausted. The director yelled "CUT!", he seemed really satisfied with the performance that I have put on today.

I changed into my sweatpants and received the payment from the director. This was one way to make some cash. I took my phone back from the make-up artist and sent the video to Alex.

I was packing up, prepared to leave, I received a text from Alex saying *Always beautiful and unique. I am proud of you. I am also on my way to fetch you.*

I walked out of the studio and waited outside for Alex to pick me up to get to the airport. It was not going to be some scene out from the movie where he would bring me to his private jet plane and fly off to the Bahamas, drink cocktails and talk about the next step to our relationship. Instead we were going to head to our destination like a normal person would do in this case, tickets booked in business class and figure out what was going to happen next between us hopefully. I was afraid to bring up something like this, maybe it was a sensitive subject to Alex.

"How are you Miss?" I turned around as I was brought out of my thoughts. I scrunched my eye brows in confusion, the elderly man kept smiling at me.

I remembered him, he was the guy laying on the ground the other day, "I am surviving in life and how about you sir?" I gave a wide warm smile

"My son sent me to an old folk's home nearby"

Just like my smile dropped, it reminded me of my grandmother, she had no choice but to live in there, it was not a torture as some old folks find it a blessing to live in there, where people are taking care of them all the time. But some of them felt bad about themselves thinking if they were a burden to their kids.

I knew how they felt, I was not even around their age, but I felt like I was a burden to my mother when I was younger.

"But I am alright there; I came out to get something from that store"

I nodded at him "You take care Sir" He gave me a wink and continued his journey. I giggled at his action; he still has some tricks up his sleeves.

Alex arrived this time in a different car, it looked like a race car, red in color and it was all shining. Impressive was the word for it. We arrived at the airport, got our bags checked in which left me in wonder what did he pack up in one of those bags for me.

"Flight 301, Flight 301, is prepared to leave in 45 minutes"

I closed my eyes in hope to relax. I wonder where we were off to.

We arrived at St Louis. It was beautiful and breath taking. "I found out from your colleagues that you loved it here"

That is true, ever since that haunting case that happened here, it captured my attention, I saved up money to come here once in a while, I had a soft spot for this place. It was sweet of Alexander to bring me here as a vacation. I gave him a kiss on the lips as a thank you and he smiled.

Alex did not hire car services yet for the day, he wanted us to walk around and enjoy each other's presence. He held my hand the entire time we were walking. At times he would stop and give me a kiss on the cheeks. He bought me accessories and brand new clothing. He made me try on dresses and buy whichever I preferred. We stopped and talked to the locals, gathering more information on St Louis, this place held so much of history in it. The locals were polite and inviting to us, most of them thought that Alex and I were a married couple on a honeymoon. Some even asked us when we were expecting a baby which caused Alex to laugh to it.

Eventually we had to stop and get dinner at a restaurant near the hotel. I was starving in hunger and my feet were aching in pain. After dinner, Alex decided to stop and watch a famous local singer busking in town. I must say even though I was tired I enjoyed the show.

We headed back to the hotel around midnight, after a long tiring day. We took turns taking showers. Later that night, I sat up on the bed while Alex dug through his bag searching for a pair of jeans.

"Alex, what do you think we have between us?"

Alex turned around and looked at me "What do you mean, what we have?"

He seemed confused, so was I. "I am asking because I think I might be……" I had no clue if I was rushing into this or making my own assumptions but I had to say something.

"I might be falling for you…."

Alex crossed his hands across his chest.

"As in falling in love" I was afraid to look at his face now, I kept my head lowered my sight glued to the bed

"Stop yourself from doing so"

How could he say something like that out of nowhere, how does one stop themselves from falling in love? It is like telling a person to jump off a building and when they are half way through with their face almost touching the ground, you shout at them do not jump! It was ridiculous and certainly unacceptable for me to hear.

"You must be confused with your feelings, it will be ok once you wake up in the morning" He gave me one of his famous smiles

"You do not get it, I know how I feel" I knelt on the bed "I am happy when I am with you"

"You think I led you on somehow?" He asked me, his voice was changing a little, and I could feel he was getting angrier as this conversation took place, but I could not just drop it, not just like that. He has the answers to every question I have in my head.

"I feel like we have something great between us, I would like to take it further"

"We can't do that"

"Why not Alex?"

"You do not need to know the reasons, you have to drop this topic" He turned around and faced the mirror and covered his face. I knew he was getting frustrated.

"I love you Alex…." I whispered

With his hands still covering his face, he answered in anger "Stop saying that, I told you to drop it"

Have I not made him happy? Maybe I am not up to his expectations, I will not make a good girlfriend in the eye of the public, and he has paparazzi at every corner of his house hoping to get the latest picture or gossip.

Wherever he goes, he has someone taking pictures of him, he has art exhibitions to attend to, many things like that to be done, maybe I was not the person to beside him, to share all those moments.

Why would I even try, I was just another dancer at some club, trying to earn money just to eat and get a shelter, why would a man who paints a million dollar picture for a living be with a girl who is desperate to change her sad life? But I thought there was something beautiful between us, the nights we have spent together rolling around in bed, those long sweet kisses, us being silly when we are together, and those late night conversations we had.

It surely meant something. At least to me……

I was starting to think even though we both were from an artistic world; our worlds certainly did not collide. It brought more pain than passion.

"I wish I could make myself better for you" hearing those words from me made him sigh; I knew he cared for me.

"Alex….I love you, I do not need a reply but I" because I could even think on how to finish that sentence, he growled in anger and punched the mirrors, leaving it cracked, with several pieces from it falling to the ground, and I gasped in shock as I saw blood dripping from his knuckles, shattered pieces of glass sticking to his skin.

He asked me "where do you see this thing between us going?" I watched the happiness and excitement earlier in his green eyes slowly disappear.

"I……" I could not even form a proper sentence for him to hear right now. I wanted to tell him how much I wanted more than what we already had now, I wanted a strong relationship with him.

"I don't see this going anywhere to be honest with you"

My heart ached as I heard him say that. How could he jump into conclusions when he has not even given it a try. I stared at him blankly hoping he would rethink everything that he blurted out. I was not going to settle for "let's just remain as friends"

I was someone that was good enough to talk to and to have fun with but I was not good enough for any men to keep me for good in life.

It did not seem like a huge matter to fuss about but it was something to crush my confidence with including how I seemed to be in the eyes of a man. I am able to go out on many dates and on each date, hoping that this particular individual would be the one, would be my soul mate because we hit off so well. It will end up being crushed with him saying "I am not looking for a relationship right now"

If I were to check up on the guy a few days later, he would be posting pictures on every social network of him and his new girlfriend.

No girl would want to feel that way, unloved. It was not ok to treat a woman in that way, no one has the right to say "she totally deserves it" No matter how an individual acts, no one can deserves to be treated badly in life.

The unwanted feeling will change you into a desperate person, to be a perfect human being. A perfect human being that wants to impress the world.

Many use my job against my love life, I beg to differ, this is also a way to really know how someone could react to it.

I got up from the bed to rush over towards him, but he was way faster than me, he walked out from the hotel room. I looked at shattered mirror, I felt tears running down my cheeks, and the same time it started to rain heavily outside. I wiped away my tears and looked around on the ground and looked at the mirror again.

I smiled at my reflection, even though I wanted to cry my heart out. My reflection seemed happy because it does not know how I felt on the inside. I was crumbling apart. I knew he would not be returning tonight to this room. I could only wish that he was safe and sound. I also only wish that he would understand why I brought up this matter, where it was supposed to be the dream perfect vacation for us. I wanted him to know how I felt about.

Was that wrong? I sighed to myself and kept myself steady as I leaned towards the dressing table.

I looked up…..

The mirror was left into pieces as I was.

I Have Wicked Games in Mind

The trip from St Louis was a nightmare, he never returned to the room, I tried calling him but there were no answers from him. I was sick worried about how he was. It rained the entire night and the next morning when I had to leave for home all alone without him. I was disappointment on how he was behaving towards me. I expected him to handle the situation like man, where he would come back and have an adult conversation with me.

But expecting too much can bring in much disappointment to oneself. When I arrived back home, I was greeted by Sharon, it has been around four days since I have heard from Alex.

The club was already crowded tonight, same old story, I had to dance and serve drinks here tonight.

"Hey! You're still here" It was Evan. It was good to see him again. I smiled and gave him a hug. I can see us being friends even though after everything that we have gone through. Forgiving and forgetting is surely an act to take up from now on.

"Why wouldn't I be? I work here Evan" I served a guy a drink but he grabbed my wrist as soon as I kept his glass on the table, I rung the bell that was next to me, the bouncer came and dragged the guy out.

Evan kept his eyes on me as I served the guys around the VIP tables some drinks.

"See this place is a dream come true" I said those words as I rolled my eyes, after spending time with Alex, I felt the need to change my life, somehow I was actually thinking on leaving this club for good.

"How is that guy of yours?" Evan asked me as he kept his eyes on the floor; I guess he was feeling a little regretful about the other night.

"I am no sure really" I shrugged Evan off as I walked backstage. I sat on one of those huge speakers.

"You have someone here to see you" Sharon stood in front of me which surprised me since I did not hear any footsteps towards me.

"Thanks Sharon, I would like to have a minute with her" I knew who that voice belonged to; I wanted to get up and leave this area right now.

"It will be more than a minute Sharon" I crossed my arms across my chest and as Sharon nodded in understanding that we needed to have a moment together.

"I wanted to say something to you in person" He kept his right hand in his pants pocket. But I could not wait for what he had to say.

"I had to leave from St Louis all alone, I was worried" I pushed his chest a little "I left you a thousands of texts and I called you hoping you would have the decency to answer me at least!" I was pretty sure I was already shouting at this point. I blinked a couple of times before regaining myself.

"I wanted to tell you that I love you Avis"

"Do not just say it and wait….what?" I was staring blankly at Alex; did he just tell me that he loves me?

He spun me around to face a huge mirror with bright light bulbs all over it. He hugged me from the back, he gave me a kiss on my cheek, something which I found him doing quite often when he was around me, I kept one of my arm on his, and took in his scent.

"I have a gala to attend to, which I would like for you to come with"

I nodded and took out my phone; I took a picture of us together looking at the mirror. I told him that I would meet him at the gala which was not that far away, I had to get changed into a dress. I ran over to find Sharon and to my luck she was backstage as well.

"Oh hey how did it" I dragged her to the side not allowing her to finish her sentence. "I need a dress, something you would wear for a pretty event"

"A pretty event….." Sharon had her thinking face on and shouted at the top of her lungs after a few seconds "I GOT IT!" she walked a little further and opened an old looking closet and pulled out a black dress. It was a long one shouldered black dress with just about the right amount of beadings. I smiled at the sight of it. Of course Sharon and the girls that were around took the matter into their hands, they surely got me all dolled up. I could not stop smiling at the sight of myself.

"The caterpillar has left its cocoon everybody" Antony's voice rang throughout the changing room. The girls and I laughed at his words; I have not felt this happy in a very long time. I felt myself growing into a better person since the last few weeks.

I remembered when the doctor informed my grandmother that I was depressed when I was eighteen years old, I was not looking forward to the medication and counseling sessions they put me through, ever since that, I closed myself, I built a wall around me. Alex was the only person who naturally broke down that wall and made me happy genuinely.

I felt my stomach aching, probably just butterflies in my stomach.

It seemed like a long journey towards the gala, I kept fidgeting in my seat in the taxi, even the driver seemed a little worried about my off behavior. To be honest, even I was worried about myself, I felt my stomach hurting and I was sweating as well.

When I arrived at the gala, I felt everyone's eyes on me, but the eyes that were dead fixated on me were the ones I cared about the most.

"Wow Avis…" I kept my eyes on the ground, I have noticed that everyone here seemed like they were Alex's colleagues. "You look breath taking tonight"

"Isn't it weird, we create memories only in the night" I smiled at him

"Best ones that is" He smiled cheekily back at me, I hit his arm lightly, and he held my hand, we walked through the gala, stopping occasionally and admiring the paintings. I took this chance to admire him, he did not seem like a person of his age, and he seemed youthful but much matured in a way.

I noticed that every time he admired a painting he would scrunch his eyebrows together and focus on the painting alone. He seemed lost in his own world. This was a bubble that he felt safe and happy in.

I also knew he kept a sketch book always with wherever he went. He mentioned if he had inspirations he would just draw it out first before he painted it. Whenever he painted a portrait, he would have his tongue sticking out a little in concentration. He hated that part of him; he thought it was very childish of him to do. I thought it was something cute. He liked taking photographs of sceneries, he felt peace doing it. He thought by painting, he could stop time. We shared a similar artistic world, I felt dancing was a way for me to escape reality, painting was a way for him.

I knew so much about him, I have noticed many things about him to remember and to adore. How much did he know about me? How much does he adore me?

"You seemed lost in thoughts" He brought me out of it; he kept a finger below my chin and looked at me "You sure, you are feeling alright?" I nodded and gave him a slight smile; he gave me a quick kiss before we walked around a little bit more.

"How has your work been Avis?" This was the first time he was asking about the club and my work

"It's all going on well, a little more disturbance for me"

He frowned at that thought "I do not wish to change you or your job, but maybe you should start thinking about your future"

I had no future Alex, I live in a small town, where everyone talks about me and what I do, and I have no plans or what so ever. How does a person like me think about their future?

"What was your ambition? Before this exotic dancing life came out" He seemed pretty interested in this rather than the paintings now. Well I did want him to get to know me, this was it.

"I wanted to take up journalism" I whispered for the both of us to hear only.

"Journalism? That is surely something I was not expecting…."

"From me? Yeah I would be taken back as well" I felt small in a way I was afraid that he was starting to judge me.

"I meant it in a nice way, you are a bright young woman Avis, stop looking down on yourself" He held my hand tighter "You have so much to look forward to in life"

I felt afraid when I heard those words leaving his mouth. I could feel something huge was coming in my way but I could not put a finger on it.

"How about we head over to my place?" he asked me as he rolled up his sleeves, I helped him roll it up neatly and he smirked at me.

"I would like to"

We drove back to his place with his slick black car, I could never get over of how stylish he was. As he parked the car, he smiled at me, gave a me a long lingering kiss and he whispered "I do love you"

We have been spending so much of time together, I felt like I have moved in with him. He would pick me up from the club late at night and bring me home with him; we would get breakfast, lunch and dinner sometimes together. Sometimes we ended up cooking at home, dancing to some old songs in the kitchen while the cake was being baked in the oven, kissing each other while we were covered in eggs and flour, until the 'DING' sound brought us back to reality.

I always reminded him how much I loved him and adored him. I would send him texts, leave sticky notes around the apartment of his and buy him things that he could use for his painting sessions. He would bring me shopping at times, helping me get new items like handbags, shoes and ever since he had his eyes on me with a dress, he made me get new dresses. We seemed like teenager in love. He never really talked about having a label on our relationship. He never addressed us as boyfriend and girlfriend or a couple. But we were like glue sticking to each other, which made a few people a little jealous like Evan.

Evan has not been happy ever since he heard from the girls that Alex and I were dating. He has been texting me ever since Antony gave him my number, asking me to leave Alex. Maybe I made a mistake letting Evan back in my life. After that fight between Alex and Evan, I was afraid that Evan might do something crazy and hurt Alex in any ways. He knew that Alex was famous and the media was always after him somehow.

I have not spent time with Sharon either, which made her a little unhappy about it. As for Antony, he was not so thrilled about me leaving early without finishing my duties. Apparently there were many customers around looking for me. I am sure they could have any other person serving them drinks.

As for the man I adore, I have not heard from him for about five days. I was not sure what was going on with him, he has not reply my texts since I left his place last Sunday after lunch. Was he unhappy about something?

Even though everything was going on just fine, or so as I think it is, I was afraid something was going to go wrong somewhere. I still could not figure out what was it. Every time I think we are taking a step forward he takes ten steps back. It is frustrating sometimes, but that is what love is about, we fix things and become better together. I did not want to be that clingy person asking where he is twenty four hours a day. When he pulls this kind of things, it seems like something is different between us. Maybe I was overreacting about this. He would call me eventually; I should not be worrying about this right now. I had to clear up my head to feel that peace of mind.

"The doctor will see you now Miss Torres" the petite looking nurse called out.

Goodness I have not heard my last name in such a long time; yes my name is Avis Torres. I had the same last name as Fernando Torres, I giggled at myself, and I actually had the time to joke around.

"Yes Miss, what brings you over here today?" Doctor Simon asked me as I took a seat in front of him.

"I have been feeling pain around my abdomen area, I have been throwing up recently and I feel really tired"

"We need to run some tests in that case" Doctor Simon smiled at me "Just to be sure"

Just to be sure? Of what exactly? I think it is food poisoning most probably. I laid down as the nurses took samples of my blood and went to the lab area. I waited patiently outside for the results to come in.

It seemed like hours had passed by for the nurse to get the results and I was starting to get a little anxious.

"I have the results here Miss, come over here" I leaned against the counter as Doctor Simon came out this time. I was looking around at the papers scattered everywhere, I did not understand any of the writings. I looked up at him.

He grinned happily "Congratulations Miss Torres"

"Congrats? What for?" I was so confused at this point

"You are pregnant! It is a bit early to confirm the gender of the baby for now"

Well the confusion was gone, I felt a little happy deep down, and I had a baby in me, a little Alex in my womb. I had to tell him, I pulled out my phone and texted him saying that I needed to meet him plus it was super important. My phone vibrated a couple of seconds later while I waited for a taxi to get me to his place.

Come on over then, we can talk.

That was all he had to say. I kept my hand over my stomach the entire journey to his place.

The guards allowed me to head up to his place, and the doors were unlocked when I got there. I pushed the door open and found Alex on his sofa, I did not say a word and went over next to him.

"I have not heard from you in days Alex" I kept my head on his shoulder.

He was reading a book and mumbled "I have been busy lately"

"I need to tell you something" He pushed my head a little and got up.

"Let's eat and then talk" sure..... We could eat and then talk, I was bursting out to tell him the news and he was more interested in having dinner.

He prepared dinner and brought out a bottle of wine which I politely declined. After dinner he was cleaning up the dishes and he was talking about how tired he was, he wanted to sleep after a long day. Tell me about it, I was really tired as well.

"Alex, I am pregnant" I blurted it out as fast as I could

"You are what?" He seemed taken back with his jaw dropped

"I am pregnant, I had myself checked out today at the clinic and the doctor confirmed it"

He smiled and gave me a hug but I received no words from me even when we were prepared to hit the bed and call it a night.

He tucked me in for the first time and fell asleep next to me. I closed my eyes, I took a breath in and let it out.

I felt as if someone was trying to suffocate me, I could not breathe, I was trying to scream, I opened my eyes it was all black in front of me, what was going on? I kicked and used my hands to push around, it was a person sitting on top of me. I could feel the weight on me, I could hear a song in the background.

You better be high on this....

Oh oh uh oh

I pushed the person off, and there was a pillow on my face, I pushed it off and sat up straight. I was chocking and panicking in fear, I looked at him in fear, Alex what were you trying to do?

He was on the floor clutching his leg in pain, I must have kicked him hard. Oh god, he tried to suffocate me while a song by The Weeknd was playing in the background.

"Were you trying to kill me?!" I was shocked; this man was filled with surprises. He got up from the floor and walked into the bathroom; I got up and rushed behind him.

"Tell me, were you?!" I could not help but scream at him, he tried to kill me and his baby growing in me. He pushed me out of the bathroom with a force and I fell on the ground. He closed and locked the bathroom door. I was afraid of this man, someone was going to get hurt but it was not going to be me. What if he used a knife on me, I gasped at that thought and got up from the ground, I grabbed my phone and purse, I looked at the clock, it was around six in the morning, it had meant Alex had not sleep throughout the night. He had so much of thoughts in his head, but why would he try such a thing on me?

I left the building as soon as possible and I did not want to go home. I ended up in front of my grandmother's grave. I felt tears rolling down my cheeks. I was a sobbing mess in front of her grave. I wish she would have stayed a little longer with me here. I felt regretful I ignored the nurse's calls when I should have attended it. I wish she was here, so that I could see how happy she would be when she hears I am pregnant. I wish she was here to help me make the right choices. I was a mess without her.

All I could ever ask for right now was for someone to hold me in the arms and to tell that everything was going to be ok. I want to be reassured that I was going to make it through all obstacles that life had to throw at me. My goals were to be genuinely happy in life despite all the other aspects being important as well.

And my grandmother was the only person that could do it.

We only knew how to appreciate people when they are dead. We are just hypocrites. We probably hated the person when they were alive, when they are six feet buried under the ground away from us, we could bring flowers or beg them for their forgiveness.

"Send me someone to replace your place grandma..." I whispered as I looked at the gravestone. "Someone to love me as you did"

"Avis, is that you?" a voice spoke from behind of me, I turned around and there was an elderly looking woman with dark brown hair carrying flowers. She passed me and kept the flowers on my grandmother's grave.

I kept my eyes on her waiting for her to say something as I sobbed.

"I am your mother Avis" she stood at the side of me. I felt more tears coming.

"I heard that you still work at that club"

"I have to, to make money since you left me" I said that part out in anger. I was angry at her. I had the rights to be.

"You should stop stripping and get a real job or you will end up like your father" she kept her eyes fixated on her mother's grave

"I do not strip and I am pregnant right now" I felt the need to tell her that.

"Do you even know who the father is to the baby?"

I looked at her in disappointment, how she could ask me such a question.

"I left you because I could not afford to take care of you; your dad left me and was caught by the cops"

"You never visited me, grandma never talked about you" It was my turn to keep my eyes on the grave now.

"She was protecting you, she did well Avis" She sobbed as well "I hope you would take care of yourself, the world is a dangerous place and people are crazy, they will do anything to get the job done right, they will not care about how you are at the end....."

I nodded at what she had to say, this was the first ever advice I was receiving from my mother. This would be the last one as well I guess.

"Take care of the baby no matter what, keep my grandchild safe, and promise me that" I could feel her coming closer to me and I felt her hand on my shoulder and it was gone after a few seconds. I knew she had left. I looked around and I was right, I held a hand over my stomach and whispered to my stomach "I will protect you first before me" and I smiled at myself. I have come a long way and if only I could figure out what was Alex's motif.

I can't meet you tonight. I am busy.

He was all over the news, his newest painting was sold for millions of dollars, I was happy for him but he kept ditching the idea of meeting me tonight. I felt sad and top of that, Mel and the girls kept mentioning how he arrived at the museum where they sold off his paintings, with a beautiful woman.

I refuse to believe what they had to say to me. I walked around the club today off duty; I could feel my baby bump growing. I think I might have gained some weight and I felt my legs turning red. It hurts at times.

"Avis! Avis! Oh goodness Avis!" the girls ran over to me with a phone in one of their hands. They showed me a picture of Alex hand in hand with a beautiful woman, around his age, with beautiful blond hair. I was nothing compared to her but who was she.

I had search throughout the internet about Alex when I first met him, but I found nothing about his life, so who this woman suddenly making a public appearance with him. There were more pictures coming through, there was a picture of her kissing him on the cheek, holding hands and having a drink at the museum.

I felt sick to my stomach, I ran to the restroom as fast as I could, I rushed into the cubicle and threw up. I felt the insides of my stomach being cleared up. I needed to get out of here. That is all I could think of. I felt the cubicle door open, I forgot to lock it and the bouncer slowly carried me up, my bump was getting bigger after all. It was starting to get in my way. I wobbled a little towards the sink and got cleaned.

Antony walked in smiling sadly at me, "You should leave this place Avis….." He kept his eyes on the ground

"Are you trying to get rid of me too?" I kept the tears on hold because this was not the time.

"I am trying to help you, you should leave" Antony came closer to me as I looked into the mirror. "I can't offer you a job with the baby inside of you" He sighed and looked at me "Are you crazy Avis?"

"I understand, no one wants me here anymore…"

"It is not like that, you have to understand" I did not want to hear any of it, I left the restroom and walked backstage and grabbed my bags, I cleared my table in frustration while the girls were trying to talk to me.

I cried as I left the club. Oh god everything is in a mess, I have no job, what if I can't find one? How was I going to provide for my child? I will be a failure. I sat by the corner of the street. I looked around as the shops were closing and there was a restaurant. I quickly ran over to that place before they closed up.

The GrillNTaste was quite a restaurant name; I took a deep breath in and walked in asking the manager if they had a vacancy for me to occupy. At first they kept saying no but as I kept on asking they felt sorry for me, and I hated that really but I needed a job. The manager finally agreed on giving me a job as a waitress while the other workers just looked at me as if I was from some circus show.

I sighed what has life come to. I texted Alex begging him so that he would meet me at my place tonight. That was all I was asking for, just to see him. Maybe he will make me feel better after all of this. I still could not put the fact that he tried to kill me at the back of my mind. But that was not something to think about right now, I wanted him to make me feel better. Only he could do that.

I left him a text and got home. I changed into my pajamas and watched a movie in bed. I heard the doorbell rang. I pushed myself up and got to the door, I unlocked it "Alex, you're here…" I was so happy, I hugged him and I did not want to let him go out of my embrace.

"I am here, let me look at you" He stepped back a little and looked at me from head to toe "The bump it's big" he seemed taken back a little at the sight of the baby bump. I could only nod at him. Later on, we both sat in silence and watched a movie

"You are here because you feel sorry for me, don't you?" I blurted that out in fear he would say yes. He shook his head and kept my head on his chest. I could feel his heart beating; I felt his cold hand on my stomach. To our surprise, the baby kicked, for the very first time. I felt a tear drop on my skin, it was from him.

I wish I could understand Alex, everything was moving just so fast for the both of us. Every time that I thought I knew Alex at the tip of my finger, I was proven wrong. He had mixed signals and mixed feelings. Sometimes I would jump into conclusion thinking that he was bipolar.

He was asleep and his phone kept vibrating on the bed where he left it. I took a glimpse of it and it was a female id on the screen. I picked up the call but did not say a word.

"Hey love! Are you coming home tonight?" I kept myself quiet as I waited for her to go on. "Well honey I will be waiting for you, just text me before you get home, I might be busy tomorrow, I love you Jayden" she hung up, she called him Jayden, it was his last name, Alexander Jayden. I had no words. I shook Alex a little bit enough to wake him up.

He rubbed his eyes and looked at me in confusion.

"Who is Evangeline?"

"I beg your pardon" He was trying to play this off and act cool, it was not going to slip away just like that, not this time. I shook my head stared at him, he knew I was dead serious and I wanted the truth.

"Her name is Evangeline Jayden"

"Is that your sister?" I asked since they shared the same last names, they might be siblings then.

"That is my wife, I have been married since I was twenty six years old" He sighed "She has been gone for so long and in that moment I got to know you"

I grabbed his left hand to check if the ring was still there, it was, it was the ring that shined under the light of the stars when we both laid on the grass. I should have asked him then but I brushed it off, I was angry at myself for being so stupid and naïve. He was married for so many years already; oh no I was carrying his baby.

I cried quietly into the pillow, I was going to be name called as a home wrecker.

"My wife could not get pregnant, we tried and tried but there was no hope, she gave up on having children, eventually I had to as well"

I sobbed into the pillow and waited for him to go on; I wanted to hear what he had to say.

"I was overwhelmed by the fact that you were pregnant, I was angry at myself for letting whatever we had go so far, I tried to you know show my anger on you"

"All the days you went missing on me, you were with her. With your wife" I felt angry with myself I kept punching the pillow while crying "You are married, how could you do this to me?"

"I did not lead you on in a way Avis"

"Get out right now! I do not want to see your face here!" At this point of I was not bothered by the fact that I was screaming at him

"This was not what you said hours ago" he smirked at me; it was all just a game to him. I shook my head in disbelief, and threw a pillow at him. "Fine, as you wish, I will leave"

I heard footsteps and the sound of the door opening and closing shut.

I sat back and hugged my knees. I loved him, the more that I told myself I loved him I could only cry harder, I was so blinded by the fact how he was to me and I ignored many important things. I should have asked him about many things in his life but I did not. I was so fixated in being with him and to start a life with him.

I adored him but I felt cheated on, more like he was cheating on his wife with me. I was the third person in their lives. If the media or this town found out, they would make it a huge issue; they will call me a home wrecker, as it is the town people hates me and now this. What was I going to do about this? How was I going to handle this all at once?

I was always left with answering my own questions. I had no one to turn to right now; I will just have to talk to Sharon. I am sure she would be able to give opinions and lend a helping hand without judging me.

I pushed myself around and got my phone on the table next to me, I dialed Sharon's number but I heard the front door opening, my eye brows rose up in curiosity, I tied my hair up in a messy bun, wiped my tears away and jumped off the bed, as soon as I reached at the bedroom, my right cheek was greeted with a slap, it left my head aching, this would surely leave a bruise.

I reversed my steps carefully as Alex ran his hand through his hair, which I could see he was starting to grow grey hair. My hip knocked the corner of the table and I winced in pain. He came closer to me, I was prepared to scream for help but nothing could prepare for what he did next, he grabbed me, he twisted my arm, and he kept his other hand on my hair, he pulled my hair backwards causing me to look at him. His eyes seemed different now, the eyes that was usually filled with life was now replaced with hatred.

I pushed me towards the wall with force and I hit my forehead, moaning in pain I was afraid he was going to hurt the baby on purpose.

"Alex, I will not tell anyone…"

He kissed my head and whispered close to my ear "I do not really care about that, the media, my family, my fans…"

He spun me around and I ended up on the floor. I grabbed my head in pain; this was way too much to handle for a night. I pushed my backwards as he inched closer…..

The sun was shining on my face, I winced in pain, I was still on the floor, I could not open my eyes properly, my arms and legs were covered in bruises, and my lips were bleeding even from my tooth. I had no more tears to cry about. I took a peak at him; he was asleep on my bed with sheets covering from the bottom to his waist. His tattoo covered arm was covering half of his face.

I crawled towards the door as quietly as I could, I grabbed my stomach in pain and crawled using a hand. I grabbed the door knob, I dragged myself up, I used the knob as the support. I walked out and I saw a key dangling from the knob of the front door, I knew how he let himself in now. I took the key and locked him in the house.

Thankfully I had my phone at the back of my pocket; it seemed a little bruised as well. Alex had the strength to do all the damages. All I could think to myself was even Evan was nothing like this, he was abusive but nothing to this extreme, Alex was surely on another level.

This is another new side to him, I think this was a way for him to let out his anger, things seemed worse.

"Few broken ribs, multiple bruises here and there..." Doctor Simon hummed as he took a look at the reports and he looked at me sadly "You are pregnant, you should have been more careful there Avis"

"I don't understand, this can't be Alex!" Sharon claimed this was totally impossible and the guy that came into my house and abused me was some other stranger, well, that how he felt now, like a stranger. "Why would he hurt you this badly?"

I wonder the same, maybe that was how he showed his love for me. I felt my phone vibrated and it was a text from him.

I am really really sorry. I love you, and you know that. I was just mad at us for having a fight.

I winced in pain as the doctor cleaned up the other visible wounds. It seemed like he needed anger management classes.

That is how most of the days went by, he would say he did not care of about his wife, he would sleep over at my place, in the middle of night, he would drag me around the house, and he would have me screaming in pain as he kicked me and punched me. He surprised me yesterday when he took a large mirror out my collection to hit me with it. I screamed in fear and he dropped it, the shattering of the glass into a million pieces was still running through my mind. I kept replaying that scene in my head. I felt as if I was that mirror; I am broken into thousands of pieces with no hope or chances to glue it all back together. Even if it was it would still leave a mark. I sighed deeply.

I had to work at the restaurant, taking in orders and serving people food, I had to do it in pain and listen to the manager whenever he wanted to complain about something. I was really tired with what life was throwing at me at this point. I was having panic attacks whenever I felt someone coming too close to me.

To top all of that, the manager had an eye for me, he would try to be flirty towards me, asking me if I wanted a raise if I did what he said, touching my head at random moments, I had to warn him that I knew people from this town that would turn him upside down if he tried anything with me.

After that one visit to the doctors, I had to start lying to them saying I fell down and got hurt or I was cooking I had a small accident. I could not let them make a police report on my behalf and have Alex arrested. I was worried about his reputation more than mine. I have not gone for any ultrasounds to check on how the baby was doing. I had to depend on Doctor Simon's checkups where he would just say "Yes the baby is fine".

I was already failing miserably at being a mother. I have not bought anything for my child, any clothes and essentials, nothing but shelter. I laughed at myself, who would know how long I would have this apartment for.

Alex would go missing for a few days, after that, he would be all over the news with his new paintings, being sold off. I was jealous that his wife was reappearing in his life stronger than ever. She was with him for almost all of his events that he attended. I had to remind myself that I was only the third person in their relationship. I had no say in this.

I wanted to tell his wife about this affair. I wanted her to know what her husband was up to. Who knew how many other girls he has been lying to? I texted Alex saying maybe it was time to tell his wife. Immediately he gave me call and screamed at me asking me if I have finally lost it, funny he should be asking that to himself.

I kept telling him that I was prepared for whatever it was to come; I was going to tell her. I ended that call and went to the club after such a long time, discussing with Antony and a few others about what should I do.

Some of them thought I should be telling his family about this affair, while the other half said that I would ruin the happiness of this family. I felt torn, a part of me was dying to tell Evangeline and the other half of me was afraid to ruin their marriage.

I received a call from Alex again, warning me if I tried to tell anyone else about this, he would get me back. In other words for every step I took he would take it higher. He had wicked games in mind to begin with.

He was sick and twisted in a way, but I felt my heart aching for his love and who he used to be, my body ached to have him with me again, my soul craved for his presence. I felt lonely without him. You know when you crave for someone's presence; you do not want to do anything but just lie next to each other and enjoy each other in silence. That is what I wanted as well.

I received Evangeline's number from a friend. I saved the number. I went to the restaurant to work my shift. It seemed like time was moving real slow, I had many customers come in today. I had to be patience, after the shift was done, I left before the manager could say something to me, and I walked fast to an alley near me. It was quiet and not dark, it had the street light overlooking the alley, I sat down at the corner of the pathway, I am sure no one would walk by here. I pulled out a cigarette and light it up. I felt sorry for the baby in me; I was almost months in my second trimester I suppose. I needed this to let out some steam. I took a puff and let it out, it felt good. It used to be a bad habit the I managed to knock it off, but it looks like I am about to fall back right into.

I took out my phone, and clicked on Evangeline's name, I bit my lips hard in hope I know what I am doing, I sent a picture of Alex and I together to her. I turned off my phone after that. I took another puff and exhaled it. I threw it away and got up. I decided to make my way home but I met Evan on the way.

"How do you manage to look beautiful even with a baby bump?" He smiled and gave me a slight hug, he was sweet at times.

"The secret is, I don't" He laughed at my answer. I stood there talking to him, I was feeling a little fatigue just standing in a place, he suggested for us to get coffee at a café nearby. I agreed and we grabbed a taxi to head there, when we got down, it was déjà vu all over, this was the first place that I heard Alex's speaking making a scene at the counter. I smiled at the memory, it seemed ages away. I shook my head and followed Evan to get a seat; he could not keep his eyes off the bump.

He wanted to feel how the baby would kick, I allowed him to keep his hand over the bump. I took a sip of the coffee and the baby kicked hard, as soon as Evan felt it, he had the widest smile on his face, I giggled at him. He was like a happy child, he would keep his hand several times and the baby would kick. He even talked to the baby and I could feel the baby kicking happily, it was painful at times. Strong kid I have in me.

I smiled at Evan, everything that Alex was supposed to do, he was doing it. He seemed like a happy father. I talked to him and it seemed like hours had gone by, we talked about how he found a job as a teacher at an elementary school, he was excited to start soon. He asked me a few questions on Alex and I which I shrugged them off, he knew I did not want to talk about it.

I checked it was around two in the morning, I felt sleepy, and Evan and I said our goodbyes, I was sure to see him again soon. I walked home slowly and as I came closer to my block I could see the dim lights in my room were turned on. That was weird; I switched off everything before I left. I walked a little fast up the stairs and the old man stopped me "Avisa how are you?"

My eyes were on the stairs, I had to get up "I am ok Sir, I will talk to you later" I pushed him lightly aside and I ran up.

"Ok darling you take care now" I could hear him shouting those words from the ground floor. I reached my floor, I could not even breathe properly, I was trying to catch my breath as if I was a heart attack patient. I saw my apartment door opened.

I gulped and looked around; I held the railings as I looked down the stairs, there were no one. I heard a table fall on the ground from my apartment. I was sweating nervously. I tied my hair up in a ponytail and slowly walked in; the place was in a mess… the table and furniture were turned, glasses on the floor.

I heard sounds from my bedroom, I inched closer towards where I could hear those sounds, and I closed my mouth I saw two men wearing a mask and all black outfits.

They saw me and let out a laugh. One was going through my clothes in the closet. The other left a note on the table near my bed.

One of them came close to me holding my leather jacket saying "Would you put on a show for us Ma'am?" and the other laughed.

I kept a hand on my stomach and told to them to get out. One of them pinned me to the wall while the other thrashed my apartment. When they were done, they laughed and ran out leaving me speechless. I could not move from where I was, I went over to the table, underneath this mess, I knew the man earlier had left a note. I pushed everything aside and found the note.

You tried to send a picture of us to my wife. This is just a little payback from me. If you keep doing this, things might end differently, I warned you for every step you take, and I will do the same but worse. Stay on the safe side, I love you.

Sincerely Alex.

I crunched the paper in my hand and threw it aside. I bit my bottom lip hard to stop me from crying. I knelt on the ground and screamed as loud as I could.

I knew Alex left his clothes here whenever he over, he would forget his Calvin Klein made clothes or his Rolex watch. When I reminded him of it, he did not seem to care about it, as he could afford ten more of the same brand. I dug through the mess that was left in my closet plus I bend down to look underneath my bed. I took a few of his belonging and went out of my block.

I dropped all of the items on the sidewalk, I smiled as I took out a lighter and kept it in my right hand. I pulled out a small bottle of gasoline and poured it all over the pile of things. I set fire to it and threw the lighter into the burning flames, there were pieces of burnt ashes flying around.

I snapped a picture of the flame and sent it to a couple of people. I continued to watch all of his priced belongings being turned into ashes. I smirked as I felt a pinch of satisfaction.

It started to rain heavily, I looked up at the sky as the drops of rain fell on my face and I twirled around in circles enjoying the pouring rain.

"This man has an issue, that's what he has!" Sharon kept rubbing her forehead when she heard what had happened to me. I sat down there staring into a blank space, if there was a sad song to play in the background right now, it would fit right in.

"What if I called his wife…?"

I looked at Sharon; my eyes were about to pop out that did not seem like a good idea right now. She was convinced with herself that this was a good thing to do, and it was going to work out according to her.

I shook my head begging her to forget about this idea. He messed up my apartment just for a text, imagine what he could do if she actually gave his wife a call. People are really out of their minds these days; their craziness was driving me insane.

She pulled away my phone and copied Evangeline's number. She kept dancing in her spot, I just gulped and prayed things would go smoothly. Plus I need to start praying for Sharon and her kids as well.

"It's ringing! It's ringing" she whispered "come on, pick up woman" she whispered to herself, I was having the cold chills, causing goose bumps to be formed on my skin. I rubbed my arms to keep myself a little warm.

"Yes hello? Is this Miss Evangeline Jayden?"

I looked up at Sharon, and she put it on loudspeaker so we both could hear.

"Yes it is, how may I help you?" I remembered that voice, she was very polite.

"My name is Sharon, I would like to speak to you for a few minutes" I kept my eyes on the phone as Sharon spoke to her, maybe this was not a bad plan after all.

"Sure, what is this about?" I could sense that she was getting even more curious now.

"Your husband…."

The line got cut off. Sharon and I stared at each other, she checked the signals, and it was all looking fine.

"What happened?" Sharon asked as she kept checking her phone. Then again, I was expecting something like this. I kept fidgeting in my seat. I was playing with my hands nervously.

"Sharon, what ever happened to that guy you was seeing?" I asked her out of the blue and she looked at me as if I had finally lost it.

"We do talk to each other, I think we are alright for now" She nodded as she mentioned it to me, so they were dating… "Marco loves having the kids around him, he buys them toys most of the time" She had a cute smile as she was talking about him.

I returned the smile as well; I blew Sharon a kiss and left her place.

I dropped by at the bookstore and looked through for some guides on pregnancy. I needed some help on how to eat right or the vitamins that I should be taking, I knew I was lacking something to do with calcium; I have not been eating right either.

I was surely a no help to my baby. The worker at the bookstore helped me pick out a few books that I could read to my bump, or and how to take care well.

I had been smoking awfully a lot lately. I knew that would bring damages later on. I paid the cashier and carried the bags outside. I enjoyed watching the sunset for once and had a proper meal before I planned on what to do next.

"Avis, would you mind if I sat down?" I turned around it was my mother. I was really surprised to see her here, the last that I saw her was at the grave and she was trying to be mean to me. I nodded and she sat in front of me. I was waiting for her to say something. "I saw you leaving the bookstore earlier, thought I should say hello before I left town" She gulped before saying her next words "What is this about a painter I hear?"

"He is a married man who might be falling in love for the second time" I could not look at my mother's reaction "I made a mistake I know... I wish I could rewind most of my mistakes" tears were rolling down freely from my eyes.

It started to rain; guess the angels above were really sad as well, I cried harder, all that emotions that I was hiding it was all out now. I could not control myself "But I can't mum, I really can't undo my life"

My mother got up and knelt down next to me, I could feel eyes on me, I could understand, if it was some stranger crying hysterically in front of me, I would stare as well.

My mum gave me a tight hug. I felt safe in her embrace but I knew it was not going to last for long. That thought was enough to make me cry harder. My entire life was just chains of sad and miserable stories that someone could write a book on and be famous in fifteen minutes.

"I know it may seem hard now, but you learn from all of this" My mum kissed the top of my head "After everything our family has been through, we are still surviving in life, that is important" I could sense that her voice was becoming shaky "I have not been a good mother, but I know you would be a wonderful mother"

She smiled as she wiped away my tears. "Are you hoping for a boy or a girl?" I smiled at my mum. Something I was surprised to be doing.

"A baby girl mum, I would like a baby girl"

We both slightly laughed, and she sat down in her seat again. She kept her hand on mine while we talked.

"I know how hard it must have been with that job in the club"

I nodded, but I understood why she left my family, she panicked as young mother, she was not financially stable, my dad was caught by the cops apparently he was involved and convicted in murder. It was stressful to process this information but I was learning about the family I never had. No one has heard about my brother, like my grandmother once mentioned to me. We both exchanged stories and shared laughter, I felt at ease.

I received a phone call from Sharon, she cried on the line, asking me to come over to her place, she had something important to tell me.

"Take care of yourself…" My mum gave me a hug and I nodded at her and I made my way to Sharon's place.

When I arrived, I rang the doorbell and opened the door, it was unlocked. Highly unusual, I walked into the house and Sharon was crying on the floor, her kids were trying to calm her down.

I could not kneel down; I bend a little, "Sharon, Sharon, what's wrong? Tell me…"

"This is your entire fault! Everything is!" She was shouting directly at me. She shouted at her kids to get into the bedroom, and they all ran upstairs, I heard the bedroom door shut. Sharon looked at me "Marco's car is in a lake! The lake Avis!"

I could not process anything that she was saying; his car was in a lake, how? "What are you talking about really, how.….did his car end up in it?"

"Alex drove the car into a lake, he asked Marco to send me a personal message"

I rubbed my face in frustration, "What did he say?"

"He asked me to stay out of everything" she picked up a baby toy and threw it aside "And that I deserved it, I tried to call his wife" She looked really sad

"Sharon how is this my fault?" I was desperate to understand what was going on

"You had to have him! You did this, Marco is leaving me!" She kept shouting at me, I could feel that she was about to cry out in anger. I knew how much she liked Marco, he treated her like a princess, and he loved the kids. But this was not my fault. I was not about to take the blame for this. I was not some person that wore super red lipstick to steal someone else's husband. She looked at me into my eyes "I hope you are happy with what you've done Avis" She pushed me aside and opened the door, "Now get out of my house"

"Sharon, this is not my..." she did not let me finish, she pushed me out of her house. I was in shock, I looked around hoping to find a way on to fix this but I could not.

Fine, Sharon tried to help it did not work out, I guess this is what Alex wanted, he wanted my friendship to be ruined, he got just that. I unlocked my phone and checked his profile; he posted a new picture of himself painting a new portrait.

I zoomed in the picture, I took a closer look, and it was a portrait of a woman. That woman was me. It looked similar to me. I felt pain in my stomach, I tried to breathe in and out, and hoping it would stop and it did.

While walking home, I tried calling the media people, people who would want our affair as their front page story. I received a few replies. I arrived home prepared to head to sleep, I checked my phone, I received an amazing offer to make this front page worthy of a story, and I could not stop smiling. Maybe the world would know about who this artist really was.

I was woken up with the smell of burnt smoke. It made it hard for me to breathe, I coughed and coughed looking around my bedroom, it was filled with smoke. I opened the window and this three storied building was on fire. I gasped as I saw people gathered out.

I grabbed my important items and ran outside coughing, but wait, what about the old man staying in the ground floor, he was really slow as it is, how he would survive this.

I ran downstairs clutching my stomach, got kicked the door he lived slightly, I kicked it harder and the door opened wide. I looked around, the entire place was burning down quick, and I could not stop myself from coughing. I was trying to recall his name so that I could call him.

Francis, yes that is his name. "Mister Francis are you in here?" I heard coughing and mumbling from the first bedroom. I ran inside and he was on the floor, I carried him and tried to pull him up, I put his hand over my shoulder and went out of this place.

The people outside were talking and some of them informed that they have called the firemen. One of the young boys brought Mister Francis aside to check up on him.

Oh Alex, you decided to burn down my place, but why?

My phone rang and I picked up the call "Avis when will you learn?"

"What did I do now Alex?" I asked

"You tried to bring in the press" He laughed a little before he continued "I could not let that happen"

'You almost killed an old man, he did not do anything" I looked at Mister Francis at the corner.

"You killed what we had! And he killed my parents" He shouted over the phone. His parents were murdered by whom exactly? Why was he telling me this?

"Stop hiding things and tell me" I stomped my foot on the ground like a little girl.

"You father is in prison, do you know anything about it?" He continued "Your father murdered my parents, the police suspected that he wanted to rob them" His voice was shaky over the line "He could not so he stabbed my father and then my mother…"

"You knew me way before the night you met me at the club" I was trying to put all the pieces together, he knew me before this, and he wanted all of this to happen… "This was your master plan wasn't it Alexander?"

"This was something that I was looking forward to Avis. But you were more than that, you brought out a new side of me…."

"Don't you say that! You are a sick man"

"I am pretty creative in a way, which is what I tell myself all the time" and with that he hung up the call.

Maybe it was time to take another approach to this; I hailed a cab and got into one. I was sweating nervously.

I was trying to gather all the information that I have just heard, Alex was out for revenge, when he said I killed what we had, did he mean I ruined the affair we had by having a baby. I closed my mouth that was what he meant. So many puzzles to put together.

I called my mother wanting to hear the truth. Was the entire time I was with Alex all planned out? That could not be true. I felt a major headache coming along. MY mother picked up, I wanted to confirm it with her, making sure this was not one of Alex's lies.

"Hello Avis, I am glad that you have decided to call me, I.." I did not wait for her to finish, there was no time for all the catching up.

"Why was my father sentenced to jail?" I asked her in a rush

"He….." I knew she was trying to cover it up

"You have to tell me now" my voice sounded desperate

"He stabbed two people, I never knew why he did it… but I knew it was only two of them"

"Do you know anything else about this case? Who attended the court sessions maybe?"

"There was a child in court. Yes! A boy, that is all I can think of" I rubbed my forehead a little hoping to ease the headache "Avis, tell me what is happening?" she sounded nervous.

"That child is Alexander" I whispered and I heard her gasped.

"That boy…. That boy you are in love with?"

I nodded and knowing that she could not see me, I ended the call. I will have to talk to her some other time. As for now, I had some important things to handle.

The taxi arrived at a huge mansion. I paid the driver and got down. It was huge; with a garden covered in beautiful flowers around, it was a perfect place to raise up a child. I could see why they had to give up on their personal dreams and it seemed hard when you have all the things near you that remind you of your goals.

I sighed. I pushed the gates open and walked in, the street lights from the corner were the only source of light I had. I gulped; the sounds of my footsteps were the only sound I could here.

I rang the doorbell and waited, there was no answer, and I could not hear anything but my heartbeat beating through my chest. I rang it again.

The doors were unlocked; Alexander stood there, his green eyes staring down at me.

This was it….

TO THE GRAVE IT IS

He stepped aside and allowed me to enter into his house; it was even more gorgeous in the inside. I could not help myself by staring at the paintings on the wall, I touched the walls as I passed by the paintings, and I came across the portrait of me that I saw posted online.

I smiled when I saw it, he painted it beautifully, and he was surely talented.

"You are here to see Evangeline, I suppose?" His voice gave me a shock causing me to jump. If he was asking me this question, he should be nervous at least, he seemed like he was about watch a good movie and doze off. "Allow me to give you some clothes to change" He walked in the front of me and I followed him while admiring the house.

He walked into a room and opened up a closet, he took out pieces of clothing and threw it on the bed, I nodded at him and picked them up. I was prepared to change when I heard him say "Your stomach, it's huge"

I smiled at him sadly; he was still the father of the child. "Want to feel when the baby kicks?"

He came closer to me; I took his hand and kept it on my stomach. I talked to my baby "This is your dad; he has never felt you kick yet..." Alex looked up at me; there was the sparkle in his green eyes that I missed for such a long time it seems.

"Your father really wants to feel you kick baby. For him please" And I felt movement in my bump. I smiled when I saw how excited Alex was to feel the baby kicking for the first time, I felt sorry for him, his parents were gone because of my father, his wife could not give him a heir but I could, I was a nobody here.

The more someone hurts you the more you will beg for them to love you. That is what I always told myself. The more he hated me the more I begged for him to keep me with him. He had my happiness in his hand, he dropped it any time that he could.

He kissed my bump which made my jaw drop a little. He stood up straight "Thank you, I should let you get changed, sorry" He spun around and walked, I heard the room door click.

It is easy to pick apart my life and to say "Oh, why can't you just leave a man like him?"

"Why can't you just run away and start a new life?"

"You could just make a police report against him"

But it is not easy when you are facing it, it is a different perspective. I wanted things to work out, but somehow so far all signs were not heading to it.

I took of my pajamas it all smelt of burnt wood and smoke. I coughed at the smell of it.

I felt a rope around my neck tighten up. I was getting chocked, I grabbed the side of the mattress, and he twisted the rope around my neck causing me to grab at it as well. "Alex, stop it! Stop please" He was hurting me really badly this time.

I fell on the ground, he still kept his grip on the rope tightly, I grabbed on the sheets of the bed, and he twisted the rope again and dragged me out of the room.

On the first page of our story,
The future seemed so bright,
Then this thing turned out so evil,
I don't know why I am still surprised.
Even angels have their wicked schemes and you'll take them to new extremes.

That song played in the background while he dragged me down the stairs. I started to scream in fear and pain.

"Alex, I am begging you, just stop this!"

"That is what I told you to do" His voice had no emotions in it, it was a robot talking to me.

He dragged me out of the house, he slapped me and I grabbed my right cheek in shock, he used the rope around my neck to tie my hands up. He carried me while I kicked and screamed for help. He threw me into the car; he had something in his hands. It was a shovel, it hit my head, and everything went black. I had no idea what happened next.

You'll always be my hero
Even though you've lost your mind

I opened my eyes, I was still in the coffin, and I was still stuck in here. This is what the present looked like, and that what that brought me in here.

I screamed at the top of voice begging for someone to let me out.

I knocked at the top of the coffin, I could feel the nails dropping, the top cracked a little. I used the mirror that I had in my hands to knock it harder. I can do this. I was going to get out of here. The cracks became wider after a while I used my hands to push the top of the coffin, it was difficult because of the soil was really heavy on this wooden box. I used all the strength I had and pushed it.

"The grave is opening up" I heard voice outside. If I was the person, I would be screaming my head off and running off like a headless chicken, the grave was literally opening up into half.

"I am not dead yet, please listen to me" I could laugh at my own sentence but maybe some other time, this just a bad moment to come up with a joke. "Get me out of here, please just get me out of here" I felt the soil being dug out, I felt so thankful right now in life. There was a couple, the man pulled me up slowly and the woman was gasping in shock.

"Ma'am why were you in there?" He peaked inside the ground "In a coffin that is?"

"You are pregnant!" She looked at me weirdly. My eyes were red and I had bruises all over my hands and legs, I had dry blood and soil all over me. I still felt the grip of the rope around my neck; I still felt the shovel hitting my head in that split second.

I thanked the couple; they have done something that I would be grateful for the rest of my existing life. In a way, they have helped my baby as well. I kept my hand on my stomach hoping to feel a kick, but nothing at all. I panicked, I was begging for a kick or any movement from within, still nothing.

My grandmother always told me that grown girls should always have a reason when they cry.

I dusted off the sand from my eyes and walked towards where the light was coming from, it was the highway; I had no idea where I was. I was just in a t-shirt, which was all that he left on me. I sat down at the side of the road side, I screamed and screamed. I was so tired with everything that I have gone through in life. They said the most faithful ones were the ones to always get tested.

But for how long?

When I turned twenty one, the doctors kept an eye on me thinking that after everything that I have gone through, I was either mental or I wanted to kill myself. I found them to be very silly, I always thought of myself as a strong woman, the independent one that did not need anyone to protect her or provide for her.

If I wanted to end my life I would have but I did not, because I knew I was capable of anything that came through my way. I am still that same strong person. Now, not only I had to fight for myself but I had to fight for my unborn baby. I could not just let Alex win this; I was way stronger than this.

I showed up at his house again, there were many people this time, everyone seemed to be having a great time, and I could see people drinking, people talking to each other. There were photographers running around and taking pictures. I was at the back lane of his home. I waited for what seemed like hours before a person offered me a ride. I told him the address and I am here now.

"Happy Happy Happy Anniversary to the Jaydens" And I heard loud laughter. Alexander saw me. I just stood there, with nothing to offer to him, on his anniversary that is. He was staring at me, I was staring right back at him. I smiled at him and he shook his head. I watched him kiss his wife, greet a few people before he came near me, he had a tight grip on my arm and pulled me aside behind a tree where no one could see us.

"No matter how many times I try to get rid of you"

"I am able to return back still, right?"

His eyes were filled with hatred towards me. Countless amount of time, he abused me, he apologized and he did it all over again. Countless amount of time he tried to end my life but failed. He begged me every time to come back to him, he said it was him, he always said that it was his anger problem and I believed him. Because I loved him so much, maybe our story was not as crazy as it seems to people. He said that was how when fire meets ice. I believed him.

He held my hand and brought to the back of the house and grabbed a hose, he aimed it towards me and got me cleaned off, he pushed to me what seems like a maid's room and closed the door "get changed and you could pretend you are a friend of mine"

I changed my clothes and walked over to the mirror. I tied up my hand in a neat bun, I wiped my face and I smiled, oh mirror, if only you knew how much of damages was done inside of me. I still have not felt any movements from the baby.

I unlocked the door, and he brought me over to the crowd. He introduced me as a friend of his, I smiled politely at everyone, I was really hungry, I walked over to the buffet and grabbed a plate filled of food, and started to eat it. I looked around, my eyes were on Alex, and he smiled charmingly to his friends, colleagues, family members. He spoke proudly about his work; I have noticed that most of the people were asking him about that portrait of me.

I heard him say "It was a beautiful mistake; I painted it to keep it as a memory"

Occasionally his wife would join him and give him unexpected kisses.

Alex was a different person here; I do not think that he was genuinely happy. He was pretending, maybe he used my mirror technique. He was always good in acting anyway. I chuckled at that.

"Oh I do not see any wedding ring" an elderly woman sat next to me, oh just great I had another person to help criticize my life.

"That is because I am not married Ma'am" I smiled.

"You're a single mother?" she kept her head resting on her hand while she looked at me. I nodded at her while I took another bite of the cupcake. "I am sure you would do just fine, don't you think?"

"You're asking me?" We both laughed and I had to ask "What are you doing here, who are you related to here?"

She pointed at Alexander "My nephew, I raised him up all by myself, something that you are about to do in life"

"You took care of him?" I was curious about his childhood, I only half of it.

"Yeah his parents were somewhat busy all the time, they left him alone at home" She smiled as she continued "He was a bright young boy, I remembered bringing home a paint brush for him, and he was the happiest kid ever on the planet"

"What happened after that?"

"His father was not really happy with what I did" she sighed deeply "He wanted Alex to become a business man like how he was, but he could not get that done"

I shook my head, I could only imagine how adorable Alex must have been when he was a child, I wonder if I had a son, he would take up Alex's looks. How did his parents have the heart to leave him just like that?

"I had no plans to get married so I took him under my care"

"He paints really well" I told her and she laughed at that, I was stating the obvious here wasn't I? "He does not seem very happy, doesn't he?" I was stating the obvious again it seems when his aunt nodded at me. But he was not like that with me, I zoned out into a blank space.

The smell of sweat of the joined bodies greeted us as we pushed through the couples. I kept saying how much Alex was missing out on by not going to clubs nowadays. I also knew clubbing was not a scene for him, he was more on the high class side, where men would drink beers in a bar with dim lights and talk about the economy and business but that is not fun, certainly not all the time.

Alex needed a change, so I asked him to follow me to the local's best club where they play famous Reggaeton music. It was time to show the latin part of me.

Alex kept looking around, probably wondering if he fitted in, the answer is a no! It did not matter now. We got to the bar, he waved the waiter over to get us some cocktails. This guy over here needed to loosen up. The Dj played a really good Spanish song. I went over to the dance floor. Alex kept his eyes on me through a gap of people. I swayed my hips and twirled around. It was all about having a good time here tonight.

It was a good few minutes before Alex joined me as well, he hugged me from the back, we did not have to jump or anything crazy because we were perfectly comfortable with how we were at this moment. He spun me around and I could not help myself by giggling. He kissed my forehead, he kept his eyes on me while we swayed to the music although the music did not go with what we doing. I felt like the luckiest woman on the planet being in his arms. I shook my head and smiled.

He inched his head a little closer to me. "Kiss me" I breathed out and he closed that tiny gap between us and kissed me.

"Do you know the gender of the baby?" That voice was brought me out of my thoughts. I turned around in my seat slightly, it was Evangeline. I shook my head I had no responses for her, I tried in so many ways to contact her, she is now right in front of me, I could not form any sentences. "Alex told me about you, I have prepared a room for you to say in here" With that she smiled and walked away.

I noticed a couple of men staring at me and one of them approached me

"You were the dancer back in that Exotic Life Club" it was not a question, it was a statement. Something that I had to lie to.

"No you must have confused her with me" I lowered my head as the elderly woman next to me begun to take interest in this conversation as well.

"I have seen you there, you danced for me" I gulped as I shook my head that sentence.

"Boys leave her alone, that is no way to treat a woman" she spoke for me.

I got up and walked away from them, I wiped my forehead and stopped to take a breath as I heard someone else talking to Evangeline "I never knew you were friends with strippers sweetheart"

I looked at her face, it was pale, and she was just as surprised as I was. I tried to act calm as if I had no idea what were the people starting to talk about. A band came around the corner, there was a beautiful young brunette woman carrying a guitar as the guys behind of her were prepared with the drum and the piano. "So, Miss Evangeline has brought us here today to play one of Mister Alexander's favorite song" The crowd cheered as I looked around. "The song is called Go Your Own Way" the crowd cheered even more, it was a famous song known by many, but this song suited perfectly for whatever that was going on with Alex and me. I am sure one of us wanted to go on our own way but we cannot seem to do so until the other gave permission.

The young woman's voice gave me chills and I began to sweat nervously, as they played the song the crowd were still chatting about me somehow, I felt dizzy just being here.

I ran into the house and went up the stairs; I found an empty bedroom and went into it. I locked the door. I sat up on the bed thinking if she would have known who I was.

I laid down and tucked myself in. I fell asleep.

I could feel movements on the bed that cause me to wake up; it was Alex sitting up next to me. He had a t-shirt on with his fitted jeans. He looked younger for his age.

I was still in fear that he might do something again, because in his eyes I should be dead by now.

"It's ok I will not hurt you" he held my hand "not just yet"

"You really need help Alex" I whispered to him

"I am not going crazy. You are the one who is driving me crazy…" I looked up at his features carefully, I touched his scruff lightly, and it felt ticklish against the palm of hand. No matter what he put me through, here I was admiring him. "You make me happy, but I cannot be with you" He laid next to me, he wrapped his arm around my waist, he kept his head near my neck.

"I was out to plot my revenge against you, for your father had done to my parents. I could not do that, I fell in love with you ever since I had my eyes on you, I knew it was wrong. I was married to a woman who did not care about me, she only cared about the money I made.

You were just a dancer, you did not care about the money I made, you were happy with who I was"

"I still am" I whispered again for the both of us to hear.

"When you mentioned you had a baby, I felt really happy, but I could not accept it, it is like my mind is set that I can't have kids not after the doctors confirmed that Evangeline could not give birth"

I felt tears on my neck; I got out of his embrace slightly and wiped away his tears.

That was when I heard the words that I was always longing to hear from him "I love you Avis" We shared a long kiss, and he made me sit up on his stomach. He sat up slightly as well and took off his t-shirt.

It seemed like I was asleep for days, where was I? I heard cars honking and birds chirping, what time was it? I opened my eyes and I was in the car. I turned to my left, "Alex, where are we going?"

"This seems like an endless game between us" He pressed on the brakes and my head hit the dashboard with a force, I winced in pain as I held my forehead.

"Well, don't you ever give up?" I asked him in anger.

He turned to face me and asked me "Would you like to be buried again? Or Should I just leave you here?"

He got down from the driver's seat taking something which I could not see, I jumped over to the driver's seat, my hands were shaking miserably and I managed to lock the doors. I started the car's engine again. I looked at him hoping that he could hear me.

"Alex, you can go your own way, I am ending this here" I was breathing heavily "You will never hear from me again, I can promise you that" I added on "You will never get away with this"

He laughed like a crazy person in the middle of no where, boy he needed serious help from someone. Because all I wanted to do right now was to run him over with this car. I'll probably try to bury him alive maybe then he will know what it is like, see if he likes it.

"You will end up just like my father Alex! Would you actually want that?"

I saw his face reaction change in a second. He had a hammer in his hands, that was what he took out earlier. He came near the window and cracked the glass with that hammer, I screamed and when he was done he unlocked the doors from the other side. I had no time to jump over to the passenger's seat to run away.

I screamed at top of my lungs, and he carried me out over his shoulders and walked into the dark woods. I kept on screaming, I could not see a thing in this darkness. I tried kicking and punching him. "If you stay quiet, this will hurt less"

He dropped me on the ground carelessly; He started to dig a hole in the ground again. I slowly pushed myself backwards.

Both of us froze in our place when we heard the police sirens. I screamed and he dragged me by the hair to get escape this woods.

I saw flashlight coming towards me and I screamed for help.

"Let her go Alex" I knew that voice, it was Evangeline.

He knocked my head on the ground and I laid there. From the corner of my eye, I saw someone running, heading towards Alex, it was Evan, he came after all, he tackled Alex on the floor. He kept throwing punches and Alex kept finding ways to block it. They were going at it for good few seconds before the cops ran over, got in between of their fight and caught Alex, they handcuffed his both hands, and a police woman came and carried me up slowly.

I stood up and Evangeline ran over to where I was "I read your letter, I am so sorry" I gave her a hug and thanked her for saving me.

Evangeline walked towards Alex "Avis wrote me a letter, about everything, luckily I was able to get her in time, she knew she was in trouble, for one last time." Alex kept his head lowered "She loved you more than I could ever love you Alex" she wiped away her tears "How could you? She is still carrying your baby; you had the guts and the heart to do this?"

"Every time I looked into the mirror, I practiced to be someone else, I managed to do it, and I hid my true feelings and saw the reflection of myself that I wanted to be"

His answer gave us the cold chills. The cops took him away.

I took a deep breath in and exhaled. I needed to get to the doctor to get a medical checkup. After everything that I have been through, I think it is the best thing to say to it is that I will learn and grow from all of this.

I sighed, my mother was right after all, people really are crazy. They will do just about anything to get the job done. Sometimes that could be the best thing to push you forward, but sometimes that could bring you to the grave. It is not just about making wise choices but it is all about playing the game right.

It is all over now, game over...

EPILOGUE

Wash wash and I have to dry it off, I smiled to myself, and Good girls go bad by Cobra Starship played in the background, which was still the theme of my life after all. I nodded to the beat of the music; they were playing all the songs from Cobra Starship's album today. I kept the plates that I have washed aside on the rack. My hands were turning into dried prunes.

It has been over two years since that incident; I have not heard anything about Alex and his family. I gave birth to a beautiful baby girl named Claire. I managed to buy a new house for the both of us; I received a job at this newly opened restaurant. Occasionally I would meet Evan and we would hang out with each other. He is still a good friend.

I made up with Sharon, we were silly about that one fight, we apologized and moved on, and she is the godmother to Claire. Antony was doing great at his club; he has many new dancers now.

As for the man I once loved, the last I have heard about him was, he is in prison, and his paintings were still getting sold out. He was practically making money from prison.

"Avis, enough with the plates, help me by taking orders" the manager came into the kitchen and I nodded at him, I gave him thumbs up as I changed my apron and walked towards the front of the restaurant.

Have you ever had that feeling where you are working really hard to be alright in life, you are doing everything to make it possible but there is an odd feeling to it like you might never make it.

It is a scary feeling that I am having right now I thought to myself.

I held a pen and a notebook; I kept my eyes glued to my notepad as I took down the customer's orders.

"Weren't you pregnant?" his deep voice asked me. I did not want to have a conversation, which was the whole main point of me having my eyes on the pad. Besides a stranger asking random questions was quite disturbing to me.

"Yes, two years ago, I gave birth to a baby girl" I smiled just thinking about her, she was a beautiful little girl with striking green eyes. She said her first word last week, which surprised me. I knew she was going to be a bright young girl. "Is that all that you'll be having sir?"

"Yes please, thank you"

I walked over to send the papers of the orders towards the back of the kitchen.

I could not be happier in life, I passed by a mirror, I reversed back to stop and look at myself.

I smiled at myself but my smile dropped instantly, I gulped, I could see Alexander's reflection in the mirror standing behind of me. I turned around to check if I was not in a dream it made me afraid when he smiled right at me.

The day I set my eyes on him, I knew I was going to love him until I die. I looked into the mirror again and closed my eyes shut.

Printed in the United States
By Bookmasters